FIRST DANCE

"I believe this is my dance, Miss Sedgwick," Lord Glendale said. He signalled to the musicians, who obediently began to play.

Jane nodded, nervous now that the moment had arrived. She placed her gloved hand on Lord Glendale's, and he led her to the center of the floor. The musicians began to play. Jane froze, unable to remember a single step of the dance.

"Relax," Glendale whispered. "Just pretend that it's only the two of us and that Mancini is providing the accompaniment." He gave her a conspiratorial grin.

The memory of that lesson made Jane smile, and she had no difficulty following along as Glendale led her through her first measures. Gradually other couples joined in, until the room was a sea of dancers.

Lord Glendale smiled at her again, setting her stomach to fluttering. The admiration in his gaze showed that he approved of her transformation. Even through her gloves she could feel the warmth of his hand and the solidness of his frame that owed nothing to padding. She tilted her head slightly so she could gaze into his eyes. As they twirled through the ballroom, Jane overheard someone saying how well-matched she and Glendale appeared. Their words echoed her feelings precisely. She wished that the music would never end, and that she could go on dancing with Glendale all night . . .

WATCH FOR THESE ZEBRA REGENCIES

LADY STEPHANIE (0-8217-5341-X, $4.50)
by Jeanne Savery
Lady Stephanie Morris has only one true love: the family estate she has managed ever since her mother died. But then Lord Anthony Rider arrives on her estate, claiming he has plans for both the land and the woman. Stephanie soon realizes she's fallen in love with a man whose sensual caresses will plunge her into a world of peril and intrigue . . . a man as dangerous as he is irresistible.

BRIGHTON BEAUTY (0-8217-5340-1, $4.50)
by Marilyn Clay
Chelsea Grant, pretty and poor, naively takes school friend Alayna Marchmont's place and spends a month in the country. The devastating man had sailed from Honduras to claim his promised bride, Miss Marchmont. An affair of the heart may lead to disaster . . . unless a resourceful Brighton beauty finds a way to stop a masquerade and keep a lord's love.

LORD DIABLO'S DEMISE (0-8217-5338-X, $4.50)
by Meg-Lynn Roberts
The sinfully handsome Lord Harry Glendower was a gambler and the black sheep of his family. About to be forced into a marriage of convenience, the devilish fellow engineered his own demise, never having dreamed that faking his death would lead him to the heavenly refuge of spirited heiress Gwyn Morgan, the daughter of a physician.

A PERILOUS ATTRACTION (0-8217-5339-8, $4.50)
by Dawn Aldridge Poore
Alissa Morgan is stunned when a frantic passenger thrusts her baby into Alissa's arms and flees, having heard rumors that a notorious highwayman posed a threat to their coach. Handsome stranger Hugh Sebastian secretly possesses the treasured necklace the highwayman seeks and volunteers to pose as Alissa's husband to save her reputation. With a lost baby and missing necklace in their care, the couple embarks on a journey into peril—and passion.

Available wherever paperbacks are sold, or order direct from the Publisher. Send cover price plus 50¢ per copy for mailing and handling to Penguin USA, P.O. Box 999, c/o Dept. 17109, Bergenfield, NJ 07621. Residents of New York and Tennessee must include sales tax. DO NOT SEND CASH.

A LONDON SEASON

Patricia Bray

Zebra Books
Kensington Publishing Corp.
http://www.zebrabooks.com

ZEBRA BOOKS are published by

Kensington Publishing Corp.
850 Third Avenue
New York, NY 10022

First Printing: October, 1997
10 9 8 7 6 5 4 3 2 1

Printed in the United States of America

Chapter One

"You'll never do better than Percival George Black," Angus MacLeod declared. "And I've never seen a more likely lad."

"Isn't he a bit young?" Jane Sedgwick asked her steward.

Angus gave her a reproachful look. "He's old enough, and bloodlines are what counts. He's got better breeding than most of the noble families in the county. You'd be a fool to let him get away."

Jane blew on her gloved hands, then rubbed them briskly together to warm them. The Yorkshire cold permeated the house, and the tiny fire she allowed in her study gave no more than the illusion of warmth.

"It's just that Mama has her heart set on sending the twins to school this year. That money was set aside for their school fees. If we do this, it will be another year before we can think about sending them."

Angus MacLeod nodded in understanding. "I know you promised her, and last fall it made sense. But it's been a hard winter, and old Hugh just isn't what he used to be.

I doubt he'll last another season. You're lucky the Squire thought of you first, rather than taking Percival to the city."

He had a point there. Squire Jones was being very accommodating, but he wouldn't wait much longer for her to make up her mind. If Jane didn't want Percival George, there were plenty of others who did.

"Well, I know the boys won't raise any objections," Jane said, trying to reconcile herself to the idea. "They've never showed any enthusiasm for the idea of going away to school."

"School's all well and good in its place, but Percival George Black is an investment in your future and theirs. We can set Percival to work right away, and in no time he'll be earning good money for you."

"True," Jane agreed. "The future of the farm comes first. Squire Jones is very kind to offer us Percival. This may be our only chance to get a full-blooded merino ram. We can set Percival to breeding with our ewes, and in a few years we'll be getting premium prices for our wool."

"I'll go speak to Squire Jones," Angus MacLeod said, as he stood up. Sensing her hesitation, he gave her a reassuring smile. "Don't worry, lass, it's for the best."

"I am sure of it," Jane answered, as much for her benefit as for his. Angus left, but Jane stayed behind in the study. It was the right decision, but the familiar knot in her stomach let her know that her heart wasn't convinced. Money. It was all a question of money. It seemed that no matter how hard she tried, there was never enough for their needs.

A chill that had nothing to do with the cold swept over her, as she remembered just how close they had come to losing everything. The family had lived a modest but comfortable existence while her father was alive, but all that changed after his death. Only twelve at the time, Jane had paid little attention to the steward her mother had hired to run the estate. Grieving over the loss of her husband, Lady Alice had been grateful to place all her affairs in such seemingly competent hands.

Mr. Cartwright embarked on an ambitious improvement plan which he assured Lady Alice would greatly increase the family holdings. He threw himself into his work, but none of his projects ever reached completion. It was just a matter of a little more money, or a little more patience, he would explain, and Lady Alice, too trusting to do otherwise, would agree.

Three years later the family was on the brink of ruin. Lady Alice's first inkling of trouble came when tradesmen came to the door, seeking payment. Mr. Cartwright's glib explanations for once failed to reassure. Questioning the servants revealed that they, too, were owed money. Lady Alice demanded a full accounting, but Mr. Cartwright had already fled.

Lady Alice had attempted to straighten out their affairs, but the complex tangle soon defeated her. Fortunately Jane had a better head for numbers than her mother, and after several days of going through the steward's papers, the scope of the disaster became appalling clear.

Their comfortable savings had disappeared, and they owed money to everyone. Drastic action was required to save the little they had left. They mortgaged the Manor and sold off most of the farmland to meet their debts. With fitting irony, the family moved from the Manor into what had been the steward's cottage, renting out the Manor, and concentrating their efforts on their only profitable investment, the flock of sheep.

It had taken Jane's best efforts, aided and abetted by her family, to scrimp and save enough to send the twins to school. It was only right that her brothers be educated as befit the grandsons of a duke. But every time they seemed close to having enough money, another crisis arose. It was three years since she had taken over management of their affairs, and they were little better off now than they had been then.

But Angus was right. With the rent from the Manor going to pay the mortgages, the money they received from the sale of wool was the only real income the family had. Investing in Percival was an investment in their future. Without the flock, things would be grim indeed.

School could wait. The boys had just turned twelve, and another year wouldn't make that much difference. And next year she would find the money, she vowed, no matter what it took.

With this resolution made, Jane left the tiny study and sought out the parlor, where she was sure to find someone to cheer her out of her doldrums. Her timing was perfect, as she found everyone else had already gathered there, in anticipation of tea.

Parlor was really too grand a name for the room, as it was neither large nor elegantly furnished. Delicate chairs from the days of the old king shared space with plain benches of local manufacture. The walls were decorated with Rosemarie's sketches and samplers that the younger girls had made. Still, for all its homeliness, the parlor had the advantages of a good fireplace, and of being large enough to hold all the family at once.

"Jane, I thought you would never lift your head from those accounts. I was about to send Bobby to fetch you," Lady Alice greeted her daughter. "Sit down and I will pour you a cup of tea."

"Thank you, Mama." A stranger looking around the room would have said there was no room for another body, but with the experience of years in a large family, Jane quickly made a place for herself on the bench between her eldest sister Rosemarie and five-year-old Michael, the baby of the family.

"Jane, Jane, you'll never guess what happened," Rosemarie said. The acknowledged beauty of the family, her eyes were sparkling with excitement. Dick obligingly jumped up and fetched the letter from its place of honor on the mantelpiece.

Jane read the letter carefully, conscious of what it said, as well as what it did not say. Lady Barton seldom bothered to acknowledge her older sister's family, and a letter from her was a rare occurrence indeed. Finally Jane finished reading. Folding the letter carefully, she looked up to find all eyes upon her. Even Michael ignored a cream scone in favor of watching whatever fascinated his brothers and sisters.

"It is a generous offer, but—"

Her mother nodded in agreement. "A trifle unusual, considering that she hasn't written to us in almost four years. I wonder what made her think of this?"

"Precisely," Jane replied, relieved that her mother seemed to share her hesitation. "But if she really wanted to help, there are so many other things she could do. The boys' school fees, or the mortgage on the Manor. It seems a waste to spend money on such a frivolous purpose." She had no idea what a London Season would cost, but it was bound to be far more than they could ever repay.

"Well, it is up to you to decide. Your father, rest his soul, always said you had a good head on your shoulders. I am sure you will know what is best."

"But what should I do?" The question was addressed to her mother, but her siblings rushed to add their opinions.

"You *must* go to London! Just think of the gay times you will have. A handsome duke will fall violently in love with you and sweep you off your feet." Rosemarie sighed at the romantic image, and Jane exchanged an amused glance with her mother.

"Go to London. We don't need to go to school, we do just fine here," Dick and Bobby chimed in together. She should have known how the twins would feel.

"Won't Lady Barton be mad if you refuse?" Katherine asked.

"Why should we care? She's a nasty old witch, anyway," Emily added. Jane hushed her sister, although privately she agreed with the assessment.

The little ones had been quiet, so Jane found herself turning to look at them.

"You decide," said her youngest sister Ellen. Only nine years of age, Ellen had inherited the same practical streak that governed Jane. "You're the one who has to go."

"Let's all go to London," Jonathan offered.

The younger children raised a brief cheer, only to be silenced as Jane shook her head. "There isn't enough money," she explained. Even at seven, Jonathan knew enough to accept this explanation as final.

"And what do you think, Michael?" Jane asked, careful of preserving his five-year-old dignity.

Michael looked at her, and his lower lip stuck out. "Stay," he said, wrapping her in a sticky hug. "You belong to us."

Jane hugged Michael, ruffling his hair affectionately. "Of course I belong with you," she replied. If only matters were that simple. Jane looked down at her teacup, aware from the unusual silence that everyone was waiting for her to elaborate. But there was too much at stake for a hasty decision.

"There is no need to decide this now," said Lady Alice, taking pity on Jane's hesitation. There were a few grumbles, but soon the conversation turned to genial wrangling over whose turn it was to help out Cook.

The next day, Jane went about her usual chores, but the letter continued to prey upon her mind. At breakfast, over a bowl of oatmeal porridge, she decided that she would refuse the offer. Her family would never be able to manage without her. And how could Jane possibly enjoy the luxuries of London, knowing that her family had only the bare necessities?

By midmorning, as she helped prepare for Percival George's arrival, Jane reconsidered her decision. Perhaps she should go. Such a chance might never come again. And she had always planned to marry, after the girls were settled and she was no longer needed. But why not marry now? Think of how much easier it would be to find husbands for her sisters, if she was in a position to sponsor them. Seen in this light, it was selfish of her not to go.

But what kind of gentleman would want to marry her? Jane wondered that evening, as she brushed out her hair in preparation for sleep. Critically Jane examined her reflection in the looking glass. Her familiar features stared back. She was pretty enough, she supposed, having inherited her father's black hair and mother's green eyes. But she was too thin, and far too tall. By the time she was twelve, she was taller than most men in the district. Except Papa, of course.

Years ago, Jane had resigned herself to the fact that she would never be a beauty in the manner of her mother and sisters, all of whom were petite and delicately feminine. It hadn't seemed important, until now. Her lack of looks would make her quest for a husband that much harder. It was one thing for a man to marry a beautiful pauper, but another thing entirely to marry an ordinary-looking girl with no dowry.

Still, she wasn't an antidote. She was young, healthy, and reasonably pretty. She knew all about running a household, and had no expensive tastes. She would make some man a good wife.

But where to find this man? The gentry were scattered thinly through this part of Yorkshire. She could think of only two eligible gentleman in the whole of her acquaintance. And neither of these would do. Sir John Morehouse was from a distinguished family, but he was old enough to be her grandfather, and so feeble that he never ventured off his own grounds these days. And Peter Dawson, the curate, was a nice enough young man, but he was far too poor to take on the responsibility of a wife who came burdened with a large family.

There was no husband to be found here, but perhaps Lady Barton offered an alternative. Surely she could find an agreeable gentleman in London. Someone who would be willing to make a practical arrangement that would secure her family's future. And it wasn't as if she expected to marry for love.

A marriage of convenience was a perfect solution to their troubles, yet as Jane crawled into the bed she shared with Rosemarie, she wondered why she felt so bleak.

The next morning she broached the subject with Angus MacLeod. It was not the usual conversation one had with one's steward, but Angus's practical, earthy wisdom had always served her well in the past. To her surprise, he favored her aunt's scheme.

"It's a rare opportunity, lass, and mighty generous of your aunt to offer to take you in hand."

"But I don't need to be married now. And even if I did, surely there is no reason to go all the way to London to find a husband," Jane argued.

"Well, there's no finding a husband here," Angus observed. "Not a single man for miles around, unless you count Mr. Norton."

Jane shuddered with distaste. Tom Norton was often referred to as the most mean-spirited, tightfisted, and surly man in all of Yorkshire. He had buried two wives already, and Jane had no intention of being the third. Angus was right. If Jane was to find a husband, she would have to leave home.

"But how would you manage without me? You know that Mama has no head at all for business." That was phrasing it mildly. Her mother had no conception of economy. Without Jane's careful scrutiny of expenses, the family would have long since wound up in the poorhouse.

"I reckon we could survive without you, for a while anyway."

First her sisters, and now Angus. It seemed that everyone was anxious to see her leave.

Jane tried another tack. "What if this turns out to be a fool's errand? Lady Barton has shown us no kindness in the past, and I put no faith in her ability to find me a worthy gentleman." The gentlemen that her aunt thought suitable might make Tom Norton look pleasant in comparison.

"I still think you should go. If you find yourself a steady chap, someone with a bit of blunt, then you'll be better off than you are now. If not, no harm done. You'll have a bit of fun, then come back home, and things will be as they are now."

Jane was unconvinced, but not even to Angus would she admit her true reservations. How could she explain that she, who wasn't afraid of anything in Yorkshire, found the idea of mixing with London society frightening?

Here in Barkhamsted Jane knew who she was. Over the past years she had won the respect of the local farmers and landowners. She knew every nook and cranny of the family land, and the pedigree of each member of her flock. She was as comfortable helping the shepherds with the shearing as she was meeting with the wool buyers in York, or discussing scientific farming methods with Squire Jones.

But she knew nothing of the grand society that formed her aunt's acquaintance. Would Lady Barton's set welcome her, or scorn her as a country bumpkin? And could she bear to leave her own family to become some gentleman's wife?

This was a hard decision to make alone, yet there was no one besides Angus who could advise her. Jane loved her mother dearly, but knew her mother would be of no help. After all, Lady Alice had given up everything to marry the man she loved. She was hardly in a position to advise Jane on the benefits of a marriage of convenience.

This wasn't the first time Jane had mulled through a problem on her own. Since the disaster with Mr. Cartwright, all of the important decisions had been left to her. It had been Jane who, on the advice of Angus MacLeod, decided to economize by renting out the Manor and moving the family into the cottage where they now lived. The cottage was too small for such a large family, but it was a sacrifice that had to be made.

Life was hard, but no one had complained, or criticized Jane's decisions. Sitting around the table that evening, observing the familiar wrangling, they all seemed very precious. Every one of them, from Rosemarie with her foolish fancies, to Michael who looked lost in a handed-down jacket of Jonathan's that was much too big for him.

She was making a fuss over nothing. Lady Barton's offer was a golden opportunity that might never come again. Jane had always planned to marry someday, so why not pick a gentleman with a small fortune? And people were people, so how strange could London be? A flicker of apprehension crossed her mind, but Jane resolutely banished it with a decisive nod of her head.

"Is something wrong, Jane?" her mother asked.

"Not at all," Jane replied firmly. "But I have decided to go to London."

Matthew Kingsley, Viscount Glendale, was having a very good day. He was returning to his London town house after having spent the morning attending the auctions at Tattersall's, followed by several hours at Gentleman Jackson's. He looked forward to rejoining his friends at White's before continuing on to one of the many entertainments the *ton* offered.

"Good afternoon, Perkins," Lord Glendale said cheerfully, tossing his hat and gloves to the butler who opened the door.

"Good afternoon, my lord," Perkins said, passing the garments to a hovering footman before taking his master's cloak. "Mr. Stapleton left a message that he would like to see you, at your convenience."

"I'll see him now. And tell Timpkins to lay out my evening clothes."

Entering the study, Lord Glendale found his secretary Charles Stapleton seated at the desk. Seeing his employer, Charles began to rise, but Glendale waved him back to his seat, saying "No, don't bother to get up," as he dropped casually into a nearby chair.

"And how did you find the auction, my lord?"

"Very run of the mill, actually. Didn't see anything there worth bidding on, although Freddie picked up a new pair for his carriage." Glendale shook his head in remembrance. Freddie, or Lord Frederick as he was more properly called, had a weakness for showy nags. He doubted the horses would prove up to the challenge of Freddie's high-perch phaeton.

"So, what did I forget now?" Glendale asked, guessing the reason behind his secretary's summons. Charles Stapleton was a paragon of secretaries, always organized, always anticipating his master's needs, never forgetting a detail. Even if the detail was one that Lord Glendale would prefer to forget.

"You asked me to remind you that you are engaged to dine with Lady Barton this evening," Stapleton said. His face was carefully blank, but there was sympathy in his tone.

"Blast!" He had completely forgotten about it. "I don't suppose there's any chance of getting out of this?"

"If you recall, last time we sent a note saying that you

had the influenza, and the time before that, your carriage broke down."

"Hmm, I had forgotten about the carriage. I don't suppose she would believe us if you sent a note saying that I'd been press-ganged and was on a naval warship?"

Stapleton tried to maintain his composure, but his mouth twitched upwards at the corners. "Lady Barton is not likely to believe such a tale, but if you'd like—"

"No, don't bother," Lord Glendale said. "I might as well do the pretty and be done with it."

Stapleton laid down his quill, seeming regretful at not having to pen the tale of the overzealous press-gang.

"Was there anything else?" Glendale asked, rising from the chair.

"Just this," Stapleton said, handing over a heavily scented envelope.

Glendale recognized the familiar scent and distinctive handwriting. He scanned the note eagerly. "Violetta complains that I have been neglecting her shamefully. Well, she is right, but I am certain that I can make it up to her."

"As you say, my lord," Stapleton said, his carefully neutral tones indicating his disapproval of Glendale's latest mistress. His secretary was of the opinion that it was time Glendale gave up his rakish ways and began searching for a bride from among the eligible young ladies of the *ton*. For that matter, Glendale himself was beginning to tire of the Incomparable Violetta's vapid charms and jealous rages. He had been thinking about breaking the connection, but then he would have the tedium of having to find a suitable replacement.

When he did search for a replacement, it would be a mistress he sought, not a wife. With a mistress a man always knew where he stood. Violetta had made it quite clear from the outset that the size of his purse and the presents he could provide were as important to her as his skill in making love. Such honesty was a rare trait in a woman, but one he valued above all else.

That evening the streets were unusually crowded, and Glendale arrived late, a fact which Lady Barton was quick to point out. As Browning bowed him into the drawing room, Lady Barton raised her quizzing glass, peering at him from over a letter she was reading.

"You are late as usual, Lord Glendale. Still, I suppose I should be grateful that you condescended to appear at all." Lady Barton gave an elegant shrug, as if to express her disdain for his lack of manners.

Glendale ignored the implied insult, and responded as politeness demanded. It was going to be a long night. "Good evening, Lady Barton. I trust that you are well?"

"Tolerably," Lady Barton replied. "Which is a wonder in itself, as I am much put upon by all and sundry."

Glendale surveyed his hostess, but Lady Barton showed no signs of failing health. Her rigidly corseted figure was covered by an elegant silk gown in the latest style from Paris. An elaborate coiffure drew attention away from the streaks of gray in her hair, while cosmetic pots provided the complexion of a woman half her age.

Lady Barton continued her complaint. "It is always the same with you gentlemen. You have no consideration for others. Take my husband for example. First he commands me to invite my niece for the Season, and then he takes himself off to Vienna."

Glendale spared a moment's thought to damn the absent Lord Barton. His uncle had some vaguely defined post in the Foreign Office. Glendale suspected that the hasty summons to the Congress of Vienna was merely an excuse for Lord Barton to escape the company of his wife. Glendale sympathized, but every time his uncle left London, Lady Barton turned to Glendale as the head of the family.

"Perhaps Lord Barton thought that your niece would be a pleasant companion for you," Glendale theorized.

Lady Barton gave a delicate sniff of disbelief. "Hardly. Cornelia Sedgwick's never been out of the country. She is certain to be a veritable hoyden."

Lord Glendale wracked his brains, trying to place the name. "Sedgwick. That would be your sister's daughter?" he guessed.

"Indeed so," Lady Barton said.

The sudden mention of an eligible niece set off warning bells in his mind. In his experience, when ladies began mentioning their daughters or nieces, it was because they hoped to fix his interest. "I hope you aren't planning to try your hand at matchmaking, as I have no interest in getting married."

Lady Barton appeared genuinely shocked. "Certainly not!" she replied. "You can do much better than throwing yourself away on the daughter of an unimportant squire."

Lord Glendale allowed himself to relax, although he was by no means convinced. Lately his parents had begun to hint that at the advanced age of six-and-twenty, it was time that he settled down. Fortunately his parents were in the country, and rarely ventured into London. He hoped Lady Barton was not going to take up where they had left off.

He decided to probe further. "The girl must be well fixed, if she's your niece." Lady Barton rarely mentioned her sister's family, but he had the impression that her sister had married beneath her station. Still, as the daughter of the Duke of Wolcott, no doubt she had been well provided for.

"Eligible enough, although I will never understand why my sister saw fit to marry that dreadful commoner. But with my sponsorship, I am certain Cornelia will be able to make a respectable match."

Lord Glendale felt a pang of sympathy for the unknown miss. Lady Barton was not a kind person, and would have no patience if her niece failed to measure up to her exacting standards. But she was not his concern. Eager to avoid any more talk of marriage or eligible females, he deftly steered the conversation to less dangerous waters.

Chapter Two

Jane breathed a sigh of relief as the coach drew up in front of the Bartons' town house. The journey from Yorkshire had taken twice as long as expected, made more difficult by the lingering winter weather. She was exhausted and missed her family dreadfully. She had never been away from them before, and couldn't help wondering if they missed her as much as she missed them. At least they had each other, while Jane would have only the dubious comfort of an aunt she had not seen in six years.

An elegant footman opened the door for Jane. He informed her that Lady Barton was out visiting, but expected Jane to wait on her when she returned. Taking advantage of the reprieve, Jane allowed herself to be shown to a chamber on the third floor. It was a proper lady's room, all decorated in pink and white, with lacy frills everywhere. True the drapes were somewhat faded, and the wardrobe was in a different style from the dressing table. But it was a room all to herself, and that made it a luxury beyond comparison.

Jane was still admiring the room when a cheerful red-headed maid bustled in. "My name's Sally," she introduced herself. "Lady Barton said I was to be your maid while you were staying with us. If it pleases you, Miss."

Jane eyed her doubtfully. She didn't need a personal maid. And Sally with her youthful grin and freckled face seemed an unlikely lady's maid.

"I don't know—" A knock sounded at the door. Another maid entered carrying a pitcher of hot water and fresh towels.

"Why don't you wash up while I unpack your things?" Sally suggested, already busy opening Jane's trunk.

"I can do that myself," Jane replied.

Sally looked shocked. "No, that's my job," she insisted. "Besides, you'll want to freshen up before you see Lady Barton."

Jane gave in, too tired to argue the point. With Sally's help, she made herself presentable, washing up and changing into a clean frock. It took a depressingly short time for Sally to unpack her things, and before long there was nothing for Jane to do but wait.

It was several hours later, nearly dusk, when Lady Barton returned. By this time Jane's initial nervousness had been replaced by irritation at the delay. Already predisposed not to like her aunt, Jane reminded herself not to make any hasty judgments.

"Good afternoon, Lady Barton," Jane said, as she entered the drawing room.

"Well, gel, don't stand there. Come over where I can see you."

As Jane crossed the room, she took the opportunity to study Lady Barton. She had not seen Lord or Lady Barton in the six years since her father's funeral. The years had not been kind to her aunt. Now, as then, Jane found it hard to believe that this was her mother's sister. Jane's mother, Lady Alice, had been a celebrated beauty. Twenty years had passed since her come-out, and nine children, but although Lady Alice's brown hair held streaks of gray, her figure was as elegant and graceful as ever.

Lady Barton must have taken after some other member of the family. Not even her lavishly embroidered gown could disguise her tendency towards stoutness, and as Jane bent to kiss her aunt's cheek, she noticed that Lady Barton's complexion owed more to powder and paint than nature. Her aunt appeared not so much youthful as well preserved.

Lady Barton scrutinized Jane from head to foot, and Jane felt her cheeks grow hot under the inspection. "It could have been worse," her aunt muttered, as she waved Jane to a nearby chair.

"Mama sends her regards," Jane said, ignoring her aunt's remark. "I have a letter from her in my room."

Lady Barton made an airy gesture with one hand, dismissing the letter.

"I suppose Alice was glad to be rid of you. Although with six of you at home, I do not know if one less will make much difference."

"Nine," Jane corrected. "There are nine of us."

"Good Lord, what were your parents thinking?"

"They were in love," Jane said sharply. She would tolerate no criticism of her family. Looking at Lady Barton's frozen features, Jane found it difficult to believe that her aunt had ever loved anyone.

"Now that you are here we must try to find a husband for you. A respectable gentleman, who can support you and your family." A sudden thought seemed to strike Lady Barton, as she fixed Jane with a gimlet stare. "I trust you will be sensible?"

"Sensible?"

"I have no intention of sponsoring you, only to watch you throw yourself away on the first penniless nobody who fancies himself in love with you. If you've got some foolish notion in your head about marrying for love, then you had best pack your bags and go home now."

"I understand what is expected of me," Jane replied, wondering if she would have the courage to go through with this scheme. She wasn't looking for love, but surely it was possible to find a man she could respect, someone who would meet her aunt's requirements as well as her own.

Lady Barton peered over at Jane before nodding decisively. "Yes, I believe you do. You have the look of a practical girl, and you ought to do quite well."

"I am most grateful for your kindness," Jane said, although she was far from feeling grateful at the moment. After meeting her aunt, she couldn't imagine what had prompted Lady Barton's invitation.

She listened with half an ear as Lady Barton expounded on her plans for Jane, and the rules of behavior for a young miss in her first Season. Lady Barton's rudeness was nothing more than she had expected. Lady Barton, and indeed the whole of her mother's family, had never treated the Sedgwicks kindly. There was no reason to believe that anything had changed.

Whether or not Jane liked her aunt had nothing to do with her purpose. Jane was in London to find a husband. An advantageous marriage would mean an end to the specter of poverty that had hovered over them for so long. And to save her family, she was willing to swallow her pride, and endure Lady Barton's ill temper.

"Am I not correct?" Lady Barton queried.

"Yes, Lady Barton," Jane replied, wondering what she had just agreed to.

"Tomorrow will be time enough to start. The first thing we must do is to see that you are decently attired. I will not be seen with you until then, if the rest of your wardrobe is like that frock."

Jane glanced down at her pomona green muslin gown.

It was one of the ones she had made herself, and while the color flattered her complexion, even Jane had to admit that the simple style was outmoded.

"Well, Cornelia, do you have anything to say for yourself?"

Jane winced at the sound of her hated first name.

"I prefer to be called Jane."

"Nonsense! Cornelia was my mother's name. It is a far superior name."

"But the family has always called me Jane."

"Jane indeed. How common! Cornelia Sedgwick you were born, and Cornelia Sedgwick you will be. And stop frowning like that, gel, I have already sent out invitations to your come-out ball, so there is no changing things now."

Jane grew nervous. "My ball?"

Lady Barton looked grimly determined. "Why, what else did you expect? This may have been Lord Barton's idea, but it is left to me to see it through. You will be introduced to the *ton* properly. I will not have it said that I do not know how to do right by my own niece." On that note she rose and swept out of the room, leaving a stunned Jane behind her.

A ball. Fittings for a new wardrobe. She had been so wrapped up in her decision to marry that she hadn't given much thought to what the Season would actually involve. Everything was moving much too fast. She swallowed drily, wondering how she would manage. She had never met any titled nobles other than her aunt and uncle. Would they be able to sense that she didn't belong in their glittering world?

There was no sense in fretting herself. She would do fine. Besides, she thought with a trace of her old humor, she wasn't the one on display. The *ton* would be meeting Cornelia Sedgwick, a different girl entirely.

The next day dawned bright and clear, and Jane's spirits rose with the morning sun. Waking at her usual time, Jane had just finished dressing when a housemaid came in to make up the fire.

Her head down, the maid lugged the heavy coal scuttle over to the fireplace. Jane waited till the girl had set the scuttle down before speaking.

"Good morning," she said.

The girl whirled around. "Lord, Miss! You startled me," she exclaimed. "I didn't expect you to be awake."

"Well, I am," Jane said cheerfully. "I take it Lady Barton is not an early riser?"

The maid looked scandalized at the suggestion. "No, miss! Lady Barton is Quality. She usually rings for her chocolate around mid-morning. Only us servants are up at this hour."

Jane sensed she had failed another test. Young ladies making their come-outs were not expected to rise with the dawn. But it would be hard to change the habits of a lifetime.

"Well, now . . ." Jane paused, realizing she didn't know the maid's name. "What is your name?"

"Betty."

"Well, Betty, where can I find a cup of chocolate at this hour? Could you show me down to the kitchen?"

"No, Miss, that wouldn't be proper. You ring the bell and your maid Sally will come and fetch it to you."

"I don't want to be any trouble."

From the look that the maid gave her, Jane knew she had been classed as a hopeless country bumpkin. With a sigh Jane rang the bell, and in a few moments Sally appeared.

After a short negotiation, Jane convinced Sally that she preferred to breakfast in the morning room downstairs. The small victory gave her a feeling of being in control. Sitting in the morning room, she reminded herself that this wasn't her home. The Bartons had a town house full of servants, whom no doubt guarded their responsibilities jealously. Having servants wait on her was a luxury that she should learn to enjoy for as long as it lasted.

It occurred to Jane that her mother had been raised in a home such as this, and at one time had taken such comforts for granted. For the first time Jane found herself wondering how her mother really felt about her present circumstances. Even at the best of times, they had never been wealthy. Her mother must have loved her father very much indeed, to brave her family's wrath and give up everything for him.

The thought of such a love brought a wistful sadness, as it was not likely that Jane would find that kind of love for herself. Dismissing such thoughts as idle fancies, Jane snapped open the agricultural journal she had brought from home, and determinedly turned her attention to the pages in front of her.

"The new boots will be ready a week Monday," the clerk said, as Lord Glendale rose to leave.

"Very good," Glendale replied. The clerk rushed to open the door for him. Adjusting his cloak against the March wind, Glendale left the shop.

Another tedious chore taken care of. Mindful of the need to keep up his appearance, Glendale nonetheless resented the time required for the endless measuring and fittings. Fortunately his secretary Stapleton had come up with an excellent suggestion. Observing that the second footman James was virtually identical in build to his master, Stapleton suggested that James be delegated to attend the tedious fittings that Weston required. The arrangement worked quite well. Unfortunately, James's feet were no match for his lordship's, and thus Glendale was reduced to calling on his bootmaker in person. But he had faith in Stapleton's efficiency. Eventually his secretary would find a match for those as well.

Distracted by the vision of Stapleton interviewing potential servants by measuring their boot size, Glendale took no notice of his surroundings until he saw Lady Barton approaching. He glanced around, but the curiously empty sidewalks of Bond Street offered no escape. Resigning himself to the inevitable, he doffed his hat.

"Good morning, Lady Barton. What a pleasure to see you," he lied, with a practiced social smile.

"Good morning, Lord Glendale. How unusual to see you twice in one week."

He ignored the barb. "And what brings you to Bond Street this morning?"

"A few trifling errands," Lady Barton replied. The maid standing next to her shifted impatiently from one foot to another, drawing his attention. Maids were by nature invisible, but this one appeared not to have mastered the trick. Glendale's gaze traveled from her worn, heavy boots, to her shabby pelisse, finally reaching her face where he was surprised to see a friendly smile and a pair of green eyes looking directly into his. My word, she was tall.

"I am Jane Sedgwick," the girl said, sticking out her hand.

He looked at it for a moment before realizing that she intended for him to take it. He grasped it, and was rewarded by a hearty shake. "A pleasure to make your acquaintance, Jane."

"Cornelia," Lady Barton hissed.

"Oh!" the girl said, blushing slightly. "I meant Cornelia. Cornelia Jane Sedgwick, that is."

Reluctantly he released her hand, feeling a slow grin spread over his features. This was better than a play. Not only didn't the girl know her place, she didn't even know her own name.

"Charmed, I'm sure," he said.

Lady Barton stopped glaring at the girl and turned her attention to him. "Lord Glendale, this is my niece, Miss

Sedgwick." She gave the girl a warning glance. "You recall my mentioning her. Cornelia, this is my husband's nephew, Matthew Kingsley, Viscount Glendale."

So this was the niece up from the country. You could tell from the girl's expression that she had no idea of the *faux pas* she had committed by introducing herself to a gentleman. Lady Barton would have her work cut out for her, trying to get this girl ready to be presented to the *ton.*

"And how are you enjoying London, Miss Sedgwick?" he enquired.

"Well, I haven't seen enough of it to tell. The parts I've seen have been noisy. And crowded. I never thought to see so many people in my life," Miss Sedgwick replied with unusual frankness.

"I am certain that once the Season begins, you will find London to be a very enjoyable place," he said.

"I certainly hope so. I wouldn't like to think that all this effort was for naught."

With sheer force of will he maintained his expression, although it was difficult not to laugh. He was tempted to see if Miss Sedgwick could be led into further verbal indiscretions, but the mounting color in Lady Barton's cheeks indicated that she was at the end of her patience.

"Very kind of you to have stopped, but I am sure you have more important things to be doing than standing here talking. Good day to you, Lord Glendale." Lady Barton took a firm grasp of Miss Sedgwick's arm.

"Good day to you, Lady Barton. Miss Sedgwick, it was a pleasure. I look forward to encountering you again."

With a polite nod, he replaced his hat and continued on. No doubt Lady Barton couldn't wait to ring a peal over her erring charge. Miss Sedgwick was not at all the thing for London.

Still, there was something about her *naïveté* and honesty that had appealed to him. It was as if a country breeze had invaded the stuffy drawing rooms of the *ton.* But he knew from bitter experience that such innocence was too good to last. Within the month Miss Sedgwick would be a pattern card of every other young lady, whose coy mannerisms concealed a ruthless quest for a titled husband.

Lady Barton stalked off in the direction of the carriage, and Jane made haste to follow. Her first encounter with a London gentleman had gone far better than she had hoped. She was a fool to have let Rosemarie frighten her with tales of haughty noblemen who were too high in the instep to converse with ordinary folks. Lord Glendale had been very amiable. His manner had been flawlessly polite, but the laughter in his eyes had made her feel like they shared a secret joke.

And how handsome he was. Tall enough to make her forget her own height, he had a lean elegance that set him apart from anyone that she had ever met before. She couldn't help contrasting his graceful carriage to the stocky farmers of her native dales. When he had held her hand, she had felt breathless. She wondered if all the gentleman of the *ton* were as dashing as Lord Glendale.

Jane caught up with her aunt just as the coachman was handing Lady Barton into her carriage. He waited patiently until Lady Barton was satisfied with the arrangement of her skirts, then spread a lap robe over her. The coachman turned next to Jane and offered his hand to assist her into the carriage.

Jane took his hand gingerly, unused to such courtesies. "Thank you," she said, smiling at him as he helped her into the seat opposite Lady Barton. The coachman appeared startled at her thanks, and Jane belatedly remembered that London servants did not expect to be acknowledged as persons.

The coachman shut the door, and a few seconds later the carriage lurched as it was set in motion.

"Whatever possessed you to behave like that? I have never been so humiliated in my life," Lady Barton said. Her diamond earbobs trembled in accompaniment to her rage.

"What do you mean?" Jane asked, startled by her aunt's sudden change of mood.

Lady Barton ignored the question, having worked herself into a fury. "And in front of Lord Glendale. Of all people! What must he think of you? And of me, for sponsoring such a forward, brazen miss?"

"I don't understand," Jane said, wracking her brain, trying to determine what had set her aunt off.

"Of course you don't understand," Lady Barton hissed. "You know nothing. Only the most ignorant and ill-mannered of girls would think of putting herself forward in such a way. What prompted you to introduce yourself to Lord Glendale in such a ramshackle fashion?"

"You didn't seem prepared to do so, and I could hardly stand there like a simpleton," Jane defended herself.

"On the contrary, that is precisely what you should have done. If you had kept quiet, there would have been no need for Lord Glendale to know who you were."

Jane was confused. Was her aunt intending to hide her presence in London?

"But he would have met me at one time or another."

Lady Barton breathed a theatrical sigh. "Eventually. But not today, not while you were looking like that."

Jane glanced down in dismay. She wore her navy wool frock, one of the few items she owned that her aunt had deemed passable, but there was no denying that her cloak had seen better days. Nervously she fingered a patch where Rosemarie had mended it after Jane had torn the cloak on some briars.

"Lord Glendale didn't seem to mind," Jane said.

"Matthew Kingsley is a proper gentleman. He is too well

bred to let his feelings show, although I am certain that your behavior must have appalled him."

Jane considered the idea before dismissing it. Lord Glendale had been genuinely friendly. He was far too kind a gentleman to judge her so harshly.

But Lady Barton did have a point. Jane couldn't count on the rest of the *ton* being as friendly as Lord Glendale. She knew that proper young ladies did not introduce themselves to unknown gentlemen. But for the last few years she had lived increasingly in a man's world, dealing with farmers and shepherds, laborers and wool dealers. It would be hard to give up that freedom, and to live in the narrow world that society allotted to unmarried young women.

"I am sorry, Lady Barton. It will not happen again."

"It had better not. If it does, I will send you back home with your ears ringing." Lady Barton leaned back against the seat, as if exhausted by her fury. After a moment she spoke again. "Fortunately, Glendale is my husband's nephew, so we can trust that he will not mention your lapse to anyone else. I had hoped for his support in seeing you launched, but now he would only laugh at such a request."

Jane thought otherwise. Lord Glendale had seemed to like her quite well. But perhaps Lady Barton was right, having the advantage of long acquaintance with the gentleman in question. Jane bent her head, as if in penitence, and kept silent while Lady Barton began to lecture her on the behavior appropriate to a gently bred miss in her first season.

Jane let the words wash over her, lost in her own thoughts. Her family was well-liked and respected in the small town of Barkhamsted. Jane knew that some of her neighbors pitied her for her family's financial condition, but she had never before felt the sting of disapproval. Now that she was in London, she could do nothing right. Her appearance, her clothes, and even her manners were under constant criticism.

So be it. Jane had never backed down from a challenge, and she wasn't about to start now. She would show her aunt, Lord Glendale, and the whole of London that Jane Sedgwick could fit into their world if she chose. With a toss of her head, Jane vowed to be the most perfect debutante that London had ever seen.

"You wished to say something?" Lady Barton asked, irritated at having been interrupted.

"No, aunt, I was merely nodding in agreement. Pray continue." Jane listened with fervent attention, wishing that she had a paper and pen to take notes. There was a great deal to learn, if she was going to take the town by storm.

Chapter Three

"Have you been to see the new opera, Miss Sedgwick?" Lord Frederick asked.

"Not yet, but I hope to soon," Jane replied. Lady Barton had been to the opera just this past week, but Jane had been left behind, judged not yet ready to appear in public. Hopefully that would change, if Jane acquitted herself well tonight.

A footman cleared away her barely touched plate, and placed a trifle in front of her. She breathed a sigh of relief. Just two more courses before this interminable dinner would end.

She had looked forward to the dinner party as a chance to show how well she had learned the lessons of the past weeks. What she hadn't anticipated was that her aunt's idea of a small dinner party meant twenty guests. Jane had been delighted to learn that Lord Glendale was to attend. But after introducing her to his friend, the exquisitely fashionable Lord Frederick, Glendale had ignored her.

For the past two hours she had been a model young

lady. She even managed to appear interested when Colonel White insisted on regaling her with tales of his military service in the Colonies. Her manners were faultless, but Lord Glendale showed no signs of being impressed.

Following her aunt's instructions, she had kept mostly silent during the long dinner. It wasn't hard, as the conversation centered on people she had never met and places she had yet to see. Every now and then one of her dinner partners would make an attempt to include her, much in the manner of adults condescending to a favored child.

"Miss Sedgwick is new to the *ton,* and no doubt Lady Barton wishes to wait until her presentation at court before taking her about," Lord Glendale said, apparently in response to Lord Frederick's earlier remark. Jane searched his words for a hidden meaning. Was that a reference to her earlier *faux pas?*

"Cornelia will be presented at the *levee* this week. And of course, the invitations for her come-out ball were sent some time ago," Lady Barton remarked. "The response has been very gratifying, considering that the *ton* is still thin of company so early in the season."

"I am certain the ball will be a crush, with everyone vying to meet your charming protégé," Lord Frederick offered.

"Then I may count on your presence?" Lady Barton asked, neatly springing her trap. Lord Frederick looked startled, but with only a moment's hesitation, agreed that nothing would please him better.

"And would you do me the honor of saving a dance for me?" Glendale asked Jane, with the air of one determined to do his duty.

It irritated her to be regarded in the same light as an unpleasant chore. Jane longed to retort that he needn't bother, but weeks of Lady Barton's tutelage had drilled into her what was expected. So instead she replied, "Thank you, my lord. You are too kind."

Glendale smiled slightly, a social smile that didn't reach his eyes. At least he had finally acknowledged her presence. If only he weren't so formal. Gone was the sense of connection she had felt at their first meeting. The viscount was treating her as he would any distant acquaintance.

But at least she would see him again at the ball. Thinking of the ball brought to mind her latest worry. "I only hope that I do not repay your kindness by trodding on your toes," she warned.

Glendale blinked, as if uncertain that he had heard her correctly. "Such a graceful young lady as yourself must be an accomplished dancer," he said.

"Actually, my dancing instructor compared me to an ox with four left feet. But no doubt he was exaggerating." Jane gritted her teeth in frustration, remembering the fiasco of her last lesson. Really, for someone who made his living teaching young ladies the rudiments of dance, Signor Mancini was proving to be singularly untalented. And there was no need for him to carry on as he did. After all, she hadn't meant to step on his foot. It just happened. And kept happening.

"I suppose dancing is one of those things like riding, that I should have learned when I was younger. Nineteen is much too old to start," Jane muttered to herself.

Too late she realized that conversation around her had fallen silent. Lady Barton was glaring at her, while the other diners stared at her as if she was some strange animal on exhibit at the menagerie.

"Not dance? But all girls dance. Just ask my sisters." Lord Frederick sounded bewildered.

"What my niece meant to say is that she is not familiar with the latest London dances," Lady Barton said with a look that promised retribution if Jane contradicted her. Lord Frederick nodded in apparent understanding, and returned his attention to his trifle.

Jane bent her head in mortification, feeling her cheeks

flush. There went her hopes of impressing Lord Glendale with her sophistication. From the head of the table she heard Mrs. Elliot consoling Lady Barton.

"It is most generous of you to be sponsoring your niece," said Mrs. Elliot. "Preparing a girl for her first Season can be quite fatiguing, especially at your age."

"As I am sure you know only too well," Lady Barton countered. "You have done so well with those girls of yours. 'Tis a pity that Marie did not take, but perhaps she will do better this year."

Mrs. Elliot ignored the implied insult, continuing on her theme. "And how is your sister these days? It seems ages since she has been to Town."

"She is doing well, although she prefers to rusticate with that brood of hers."

"Such a pity that she doesn't visit London more often. The last time I saw her was before her marriage. What a beauty she was. She could have had any gentleman in the *ton*. Even my Harry was part of her court for a while, as was Lord Barton."

"Nonsense," Lady Barton replied stiffly. "Alice was pretty, I will grant you that, but hardly a reigning beauty. And Barton was far too intelligent to trail after such a fickle miss."

"As you say," said Mrs. Elliot. "Although I remember it differently."

Jane forgot her mortification, intrigued by Mrs. Elliot's revelations. To think that Lord Barton had been one of her mother's beaux. No wonder Lady Barton still resented her sister. With two beautiful sisters herself, Jane could feel sympathy for Lady Barton's plight. She wondered if Lady Barton had always been caustic and bitter, or if she had become so out of disappointment.

The rest of the dinner passed without incident, and the ladies retired to the drawing room. Jane found herself seated next to the outspoken Mrs. Elliot, who questioned

Jane closely about her family. Jane confined her replies to the vaguest of generalities, not wanting to reveal their circumstances. Mrs. Elliot proved persistent, so it was with relief that Jane greeted the arrival of the gentlemen.

To her delight, Lord Glendale and Lord Frederick chose to lounge against the mantelpiece, next to where she was sitting. Soon after Mrs. Elliot rose and went over to talk with another member of the party, leaving Jane alone on the bench.

"Lord Glendale," she began, "I must apologize for my remarks earlier. I spoke without thinking."

"No need to apologize," Lord Glendale replied. "Although, I trust you were exaggerating."

Jane looked around, making sure that no one else was within earshot. "I am afraid not. There is so much to learn, and it seems the harder I try the worse I get. I don't know how I can possibly be ready in time for the ball." It was a relief to confide in someone.

"But surely you have been to assemblies before. Even if you know only the country dances, it will be enough."

Didn't he hear what she was saying? "What I meant was that I don't know *any* of the dances. I have never been to an assembly, so there was never any reason for me to learn."

Gone was the carefully cultivated mask of boredom. Lord Glendale was grinning when he asked, "Never?"

"Never," she affirmed. "Unless you count the shearing festival? Just last spring I persuaded Angus MacLeod to show us some Scottish dances. Very energetic they were. But I don't suppose the Highland jig is popular in London?"

"Indeed not," Glendale replied. He started to laugh and then attempted to cover it by coughing. Once started he could not stop, and Lord Frederick began to helpfully pound him on the back. Glendale only laughed harder.

Jane glared furiously at the pair. How dare they mock

her? Was this how Lord Glendale treated his friends? She could feel her aunt's gaze boring holes in her back, but refused to turn around to acknowledge her censure. She waited until Glendale had himself under control, and then rose unhurriedly from her seat. With a stiff nod to the gentlemen, Jane retreated to the far side of the room, where she stayed next to her aunt for the rest of the evening.

"Well, that was a deuced dull evening," Lord Frederick remarked, climbing into the carriage. "Can't imagine why you dragged me along."

Glendale eased himself back against the velvet squabs, stretching his long legs with a sense of relief. "But I needed you, Freddie. Would you have condemned me to face Lady Barton on my own? My heart quakes at the thought."

Freddie gave a snort of disdain. "Don't try to gammon me. There isn't a woman alive who could frighten you. No, you were expecting another one of Lady Barton's tediously proper entertainments, and refused to suffer alone."

"As you say," Glendale agreed. "But the night is still young. I promised you a round of cards at White's, did I not? Or we could seek more convivial company."

"White's by all means," Freddie agreed.

Glendale gave the necessary instructions to the driver. As the carriage started off, he gazed at his companion. Lord Frederick was a good friend. They had much in common, having both assumed their titles and family responsibilities at an early age, when their contemporaries were still sowing their wild oats. But whereas Glendale had never had any trouble commanding respect, Freddie was cursed with boyish good looks and an obliging nature. Strangers took one look at Freddie's cheerful round face and immediately assumed that he was a decade younger than his actual age.

With ladies it was worse, for they treated Freddie as a younger brother or favorite nephew, and took advantage of his good nature.

In his quest to appear a gentleman of consequence, Freddie had lately taken to a passionate following of the latest fashions. Tonight was no exception. His dark blue coat and black silk breeches were unexceptionable on their own, but Frederick had chosen a red- and yellow-striped waistcoat to set them off. Not content there, he wore enough fobs, seals, and pins to make the fingers of any pickpocket itch.

Glendale was one of the few who realized that beneath the dandyish exterior lay a capable brain. Even if Freddie did have the unfortunate habit of always speaking his mind.

As he was doing now. "That niece of Lady Barton's was quite the surprise," Frederick commented. "Lady Barton will have her hands full with that one."

"Miss Sedgwick was quite lively," Glendale observed diplomatically.

"Lively!" Freddie gave a bark of laughter. "Hoydenish is more like it. She'll never last a week if she doesn't learn to watch that tongue of hers. Never been to a dance indeed."

Glendale felt compelled to defend the absent Miss Sedgwick. "All she needs is to acquire some town bronze, and she will do quite well. Even you must admit that she looked fetching this evening."

Indeed he had hardly recognized her. Miss Sedgwick had been striking, in a pale blue gown that showed her youthful figure to advantage. Her ebony tresses, piled high for the occasion, set off her creamy white skin. She was not a beauty in the accepted mode, but he had found himself captivated.

"Fetching? I suppose, if you have a taste for Long Megs. Not all of us are giants like yourself. No, the chit is much too tall to be fashionable, and much too gauche to last the Season. I'll wager that Miss Sedgwick will be packed off to the country in a month."

"Done," said Glendale, recklessly. "I'll wager you a hundred pounds that she lasts the month." It would be a shame if Miss Sedgwick left Town. He had been looking forward to watching her maneuver her way through the Season.

Freddie straightened out of his careless sprawl and extended his hand across the carriage. "I'll enjoy taking your money, Glendale. This is one wager I can't lose."

The next morning dawned fresh and clear, bringing the illusion of a country spring to the busy metropolis. Matthew Kingsley stood on the steps of his family's town house, pausing a moment to savor the sunshine on his face, after so many weeks of cold and rain. If it weren't for the noise of rattling carriages and crying hawkers, he could almost imagine himself back in the country.

Thoughts of the country led to thoughts of last night's dinner, and Miss Sedgwick. And to that foolish wager. He had accepted on impulse, feeling an unexplainable need to defend her.

He and Freddie had proceeded with due solemnity to White's, where Freddie, somewhat the worse for the bottles of brandy they had consumed, entered the wager into the betting books. Even before the ink was dry, Glendale had begun to regret his acceptance. He had no chance of winning. He might as well write Freddie a draft for the hundred pounds now and be done with it.

Perhaps there was a way he could increase the odds in his favor. Pausing before climbing into the waiting carriage, he called up to the driver. "Gardner, I've changed my mind. Take me to the Bartons."

"As you wish, my lordship," the coachman replied.

As the coach moved off, Glendale congratulated himself

on his inspiration. Cornelia Sedgwick was about to become the toast of London. With his help, of course. All the chit needed was a firm hand to show her the way. And he would have the satisfaction of outwitting Lord Frederick yet again.

"Lady Barton is not at home, my lord. Shall I tell her that you called?" Browning suggested, with the grave tones of someone imparting a state secret. Years of being in Lady Barton's employ had rubbed off on the man, to the point where the butler had a vastly inflated idea of his own consequence. Normally Glendale enjoyed baiting the staid butler, but today he had far more important things on his mind.

"Is Miss Sedgwick at home?"

Browning hesitated, glancing upstairs to where the strains of music could be heard, before replying, "Miss Sedgwick is not receiving visitors."

A crash sounded from above, followed by the sound of someone cursing in broken Italian.

"I see Miss Sedgwick is having her dance lesson," Glendale observed, handing his hat and gloves to Browning. Shrugging off his cape, he headed towards the stairs before the officious butler could react.

"But, my lord!" Browning exclaimed. "I have specific instructions from Lady Barton. Miss Sedgwick is not to receive visitors."

No doubt Lady Barton hoped to smooth some more of the rough edges off her charge before allowing her to mix with society.

"I am certain that she did not mean to exclude me. After all, I am family."

Running up the stairs two at a time, he soon reached the music room and the source of the commotion. He had guessed correctly. Miss Sedgwick was there, looking not at all repentant as a middle-aged gentleman lectured her, gesticulating wildly.

"Mees Sedgwick, I tell you once, I tell you again. Graceful. You must skip lightly. Like a deer. Or a goat. Not stomp like—like elephant!" The instructor spotted Glendale and turned to him for aid. "See? Here is a man who knows. You tell her, sir. Tell her that young ladies do not stick their big feet out to trip the gentlemen."

"How do you expect me to concentrate when you are always yelling at me? If you would just be quiet, I am sure I could figure this out. Are you certain that you've never had any problems with the girls you've taught before?" Miss Sedgwick countered. "Oh, good morning, Lord Glendale," she said, belatedly acknowledging his presence.

"Good morning, Miss Sedgwick," he replied politely. "I trust that I am not intruding?"

"No, no, I am certain Signor Mancini is grateful for the interruption."

Glendale looked at her enquiringly, and Miss Sedgwick rushed to complete the introductions.

"Lord Glendale, this is Signor Mancini, who is attempting to teach me the rudiments of dance. And Mrs. Mancini, who has condescended to play the pianoforte for us this morning."

Mrs. Mancini seemed overwhelmed by his presence, rising and curtseying nervously. Signor Mancini took things in stride, bowing jerkily and proclaiming, "I, Mancini, am at your service, your lordship. Tell me how Mancini can be of assistance."

Glendale winced at the comic opera accent. He had never heard anything like it, not even during his sojourn in Italy. From their looks the Mancinis hailed from no further south than South London, but no doubt the accent was part of their professional image.

"Do not let me disturb you," he said, with an airy wave of his hand. "Pray continue with the lesson."

Miss Sedgwick shot him a reproachful look, before assuming her place in the center of the floor. Glendale snagged a nearby chair from against the wall, and sat down to watch the spectacle.

Mrs. Mancini resumed her seat at the pianoforte, as her husband took his place opposite Miss Sedgwick. They made an odd sight, as Signor Mancini was at least a foot shorter than Miss Sedgwick. The poor man's head was tilted back at an angle, for if he looked straight ahead, he would be gazing at Miss Sedgwick's well-endowed bosom.

"We will go back and begin again," Mancini instructed. "And one and two and . . ."

Judging from the expression on her face, Miss Sedgwick was concentrating fiercely. She began the dance well enough, but began to lose her place under the constant barrage of instructions from Mancini.

"And turn left, no *left,* and head up, and smile, and watch your arms, and hop, and back to place, and advance, and look up, not at the feet—"

The last instruction was ill timed, as Miss Sedgwick, dutifully looking up, advanced towards her partner with such diligence that she stomped on his foot.

"Blast it!" Mancini wailed, hopping around on one foot, while holding the other with his hand. The music trailed off uncertainly in the background. " 'Aven't you 'eard a word that I said? Or did you think I was just yammering for me 'ealth?"

Signor Mancini's veneer of sophistication was cracking, and Glendale judged it time to intervene.

"May I offer a suggestion?" Glendale said.

"No," Miss Sedgwick replied, with an air of injured dignity. "Not unless you know of another caper merchant. Preferably one with fewer sensibilities."

Signor Mancini placed his injured foot back on the ground, and regarded Glendale with a look of desperation.

"My lord? You see how hard Mancini work. Miss Sedgwick is difficult, yes, but Mancini will manage."

The idea of a new instructor had merit. Miss Sedgwick would never learn anything under that constant barrage of criticism. About to agree, he glanced over to where Mrs. Mancini sat at the pianoforte. Mrs. Mancini averted her eyes, but her white face and set expression told their own story. Heaven knew where Lady Barton had found these two, but it was clear that the Mancinis could not afford to lose this student.

The Mancinis' problems were no worry of his, but somehow he couldn't bring himself to turn them off. It was not an act of kindness on his part, but mere practicality. After all, the dance was in just a few days. It would be difficult to find another instructor before then, and who knew if the new one would prove any better than the old.

"Well?" Miss Sedgwick prompted.

There was no other choice. "Why don't I take a turn?" he suggested, rising from the chair.

"You?"

There was no reason for her to sound so surprised. "Me. After all, you promised me that dance. I have to be certain that you won't disgrace me."

Jane swallowed nervously, wiping suddenly damp palms on the skirt of her gown. Having Lord Glendale witness her earlier humiliation was bad enough, but this was impossible. What if she tripped him up? She would never be able to face him again.

Glendale took his place opposite her. From a distance she was aware that Signor Mancini had replaced his wife at the pianoforte.

"Are you certain that you want to do this?"

"Relax," he said, giving her a brilliant smile. "Trust me. I've done this before you know."

Jane gathered the shreds of her confidence. She essayed a weak smile in return.

"Besides," he said. "Unlike Mancini, I am wearing riding boots. You can't possibly harm me."

How dare he poke fun at her. Jane glared at him, no longer afraid. The music began, and Jane curtseyed to her partner. She began the steps, paying no attention to her feet, instead keeping her gaze fixed on Glendale's face. The man had the gall to look as if he were enjoying himself. To her surprise, the figures of the dance flew by.

It was a pleasure to dance with Glendale. It was not just that he didn't have to crane his neck to look into her eyes. His steady gaze was filled with admiration and his smile held the warmth of long friendship. He made her feel special, as if there was nothing that he would rather be doing than dancing with her.

She faltered only once, looking down at her feet when she reached the point where she had tripped the hapless Mancini.

"You are doing fine," Glendale reassured her. She looked back at him in surprise, realizing the truth of his words. She wasn't a hopeless case, after all. With renewed self-confidence she continued the rest of the dance.

The music stopped and Jane blinked, reluctant to have this moment come to an end. "That was wonderful!"

"It was nothing," Glendale replied. "You just needed someone with a bit more experience to show you the way." He extended his arm to her.

Jane hesitated, then placed her hand tentatively on his arm. She could feel his powerful muscles under the fabric of his coat. Her hand tingled from the contact. His nearness affected her in ways she didn't understand. Looking up at his chiseled features and wavy brown hair, she realized just how devastatingly attractive he was. She had been thinking of him as a friend, but mere friendship did not explain why it felt so good when he held her in his arms.

She wondered if he felt the same way about her, and then dismissed the thought as foolish fancy. She wasn't the first young woman he had danced with. In his years on the town he must have had dozens or even hundreds of elegant and sophisticated ladies vying for his attention. Which made it odd that he had never married. Perhaps he was the sort of man who found it impossible to limit his attentions to one woman.

Mancini's effusive compliments kept her from pursuing the thought further, as he said, "Oh, your lordship, that was perfection itself. Such elegance! Such style! With such a partner, how could Miss Sedgwick be anything but graceful?"

Jane hurriedly removed her hand from Glendale's arm.

Glendale frowned at the interruption, but when he turned to Mancini his tone was all politeness. "I have no doubt that Miss Sedgwick will soon be an accomplished dancer, under your fine tutelage."

Mancini preened under the compliment.

"And now, Miss Sedgwick, I must take my leave."

"So soon?" It seemed he had just arrived, although a glance at the wall clock showed he had been there for almost an hour. Jane couldn't help feeling disappointed, even though she knew that Glendale surely had more important things to do than to wait on her.

"Yes, I only stopped in for a moment."

"Well I am sorry you must leave, but I will not keep you. Please accept my thanks for calling," Jane said. "I don't know how we would have managed without you."

Glendale smiled at her, a devastating smile that must have captured a thousand hearts. "The pleasure was all mine, Miss Sedgwick." He took her hand in his and raised it to his lips for a kiss. Jane blushed furiously at his gallantry.

"Perhaps I could call again later this week to see how you are progressing? And to pay my respects to Lady Barton, of course."

"That would be most kind," Jane replied, hoping fervently that Lady Barton would not be at home when he called. She knew instinctively that Lady Barton would never have approved of the impromptu dance lesson.

Glendale bowed, and Mancini escorted him to the door where they exchanged parting words. Mancini returned and resumed the lesson with a new spirit of enthusiasm. Glendale's influence must have done some good, for Mancini kept his comments to a minimum, and Jane made only a few mistakes. But it was not the same. The excitement had departed with Glendale, and she wished that he would return.

Chapter Four

"Wasn't the *levee* just too terrifying? I vow, when the equerry announced my name, I thought I would die on the spot," Miss Blake confided.

Jane nodded, her patience showing signs of strain around the edges as Miss Blake continued to prattle on. When Browning had ushered Miss Blake and her mother into the morning room, Miss Blake had hurried for the empty chair next to Jane's. Miss Blake declared herself thrilled to see Jane again, claiming to remember her from their mutual presentation to the Queen.

Jane's chief impression of that afternoon was her relief when it was over. She had felt ridiculous in the old-fashioned court dress with its wide-hooped skirts and plumed head-dress. But the Queen was reputed to be very strict about such things, and Jane had the comfort of seeing that all the other young ladies were similarly attired.

What Jane remembered most was the tedium. The ante-chamber had been packed with people, the heat adding to the discomfort of the gown. The room was filled with young ladies, who all seemed to have known each other since the cradle. A kindhearted girl, hardly older than Rosemarie, had attempted to engage Jane in conversation, but it soon became apparent that they had nothing in common.

By the time it was her turn, Jane had ceased to be nervous. She just wanted to get it over with. She entered the receiving room, walking with care so as not to trip over the hoops. She approached the Queen, and then made an elegant curtsey. The Queen nodded, and the attendant signalled Jane to rise. Jane backed out of the room, feeling a sense of anticlimax. It had hardly seemed worth all the fuss.

"And isn't the Season too wonderful!" Miss Blake exclaimed. "I haven't slept for a week. Every night there is something exciting to do. Some nights we go to two or three different events, and we still must turn down over half the invitations we receive."

Jane's only outing so far had consisted of a musicale, where her musical sensibilities had been outraged by the fumble-fingered efforts of the hostess's two daughters. The Italian tenor who followed had not been much better, but he was very good-looking in a dark-complexioned way, which no doubt accounted for his popularity.

"It has been quite interesting," Jane agreed diplomatically.

"The only disappointment was Almack's. Have you been there?" Miss Blake continued on, not waiting for a response. "I never saw so many handsome gentlemen in my life. Everyone was so elegant, but the rooms were quite shabby. Why the assembly rooms back home are more refined."

Out of the corner of her eye, Jane could see Mrs. Dunne approaching. Having met Mrs. Dunne previously, and endured a long lecture on the sad lack of manners among younger ladies, Jane was in no mood to listen to another tirade. Turning back to Miss Blake she said, "You must tell me all about it, for Lady Sefton has been kind enough to send us vouchers."

Miss Blake obliging launched into a vaguely coherent description of Almack's. Jane listened with half an ear, nodding and agreeing whenever her companion paused for breath. Mrs. Dunne passed them by, choosing a seat next to the elderly Miss Gunther. But now Jane was trapped by her own cleverness, as Miss Blake continued to rattle on. When the door opened Jane looked up, hoping for a diversion.

"Lord Glendale," Browning intoned importantly.

Glendale came striding through the door, making his way over to Lady Barton. His graceful and unhurried movements, coupled with his lean muscular body, gave the impression of barely leashed energy. Conversation ceased, and Lady Barton's callers began to preen, as if waiting to see where his attention would fall. Out of the corner of her eye, Jane saw Miss Blake surreptitiously rearrange the folds of her gown, and then fix a bright smile on her face.

"Good morning, Lady Barton," he said, bending to kiss her cheek. "I trust I find you well."

"Well enough," Lady Barton said, visibly triumphant at having such a distinguished caller. "And what brings you here this morning?"

"It is such a beautiful day, I thought Miss Sedgwick would enjoy a drive in the park," Glendale said, looking over to where she sat.

Jane jumped up, eager to escape. "How very kind of you, sir," she replied. Then, mindful of her manners, she looked to Lady Barton for permission.

Lady Barton nodded regally. If she was disappointed that Lord Glendale had no intention of staying, she did not show it.

"I will be ready in a moment," Jane said to Glendale.

Taking her leave of the callers, she walked with the appearance of calmness to the hall.

The hall was empty, and Jane raced up the stairs to her room. Sally was nowhere in sight, so Jane threw open the doors of her wardrobe. Dresses of all descriptions crammed the wardrobe, and Jane blinked at the evidence of her aunt's unlikely generosity.

How did Sally ever find anything? Recklessly shoving aside the expensive garments, she finally found the cloaks in the back. Her hand hesitated over the blue. The merino spencer was elegant, but much too fine for such a cold day. The emerald green wool then. The dressmaker had said it matched her eyes. She wondered if Lord Glendale would notice how becoming it was.

Grabbing the matching bonnet from the overhead shelf, Jane threw on the cloak and tied the bonnet. She paused to check her appearance in the glass. Passable enough, she supposed. Then she hurried down the stairs, to find Glendale waiting for her.

"Ready so soon?" he asked.

She nodded. "Let us leave before Lady Barton changes her mind."

Glendale handed Miss Sedgwick into the curricle, then sprang up beside her. He took the reins from the groom, and waited until the man climbed onto the back seat before driving off with a flourish.

"It seems you have rescued me again, my lord," Miss Sedgwick said. "I don't know how much longer I could have managed to sit there and make polite conversation about nothing."

Glendale sympathized with her. He had thought to pay a morning call to check on Miss Sedgwick's progress, but hadn't taken into account that the London Season was now in earnest. Lady Barton's morning room had been packed with eligible young ladies and their doting mamas. Only his quick wits in suggesting the drive had saved him.

If the weather had been rainy, he would have been trapped in that room. The prospect was enough to make any carefree bachelor break into a cold sweat.

"Delighted that I could be of service. And it is far too lovely a day to spend it indoors."

"I would have braved a Yorkshire blizzard, just to escape that crowd. And from the expression on your face when you entered, I suggest you felt the same."

Glendale was still pondering his narrow escape. "Did you see that room? Nothing but eligible young ladies and their mothers. Were I to pay the slightest of attentions to any of those girls, she would construe it as a declaration, and her parents would send the notice to the papers."

"And where does that leave me?" Miss Sedgwick asked.

Glendale glanced over to Miss Sedgwick, startled by her perception. He must remember not to underestimate her. Her ignorance of *ton* manners did not mean that she was lacking in wit. He thought furiously for a moment. He could hardly tell her about that absurd wager with Lord Frederick.

"Well, that's different . . ."

Miss Sedgwick arched her eyebrows, indicating her disbelief. "Go on," she prompted.

Inspiration struck. "You are family. We are cousins, of a sort." He hurried on with his explanation. "After all, Lady Barton is your aunt, and she is my uncle's wife."

"Cousins," she repeated wonderingly. "I never thought of it that way."

She appeared satisfied with this explanation, and Glendale allowed himself to relax.

"In that case you must call me Cousin Jane," she said.

He smiled, remembering their first introduction. "Jane? I thought Lady Barton introduced you as Cornelia?"

"Bah! I hate that name. No one calls me Cornelia except Lady Barton, and she does it only to spite me. If we're to be friends, you will call me Jane."

Friends. Well, why not? He had never had a friend who was a woman before, but that didn't mean it wasn't possible. And Miss Sedgwick certainly didn't fit any of the other categories of women that he was familiar with.

"Very well," he said, shaking her hand to seal the bargain. "Friends it is, Cousin Jane. And you can call me Matthew."

On that note, they reached Green Park. It was the perfect place for his purposes, fashionable enough, but far less crowded than Hyde Park. In Green Park it was possible to drive more than ten yards without being hailed by an acquaintance.

Miss Sedgwick was suitably impressed. "It's so lovely," she exclaimed. "I didn't know there was anything like this in London. It seems like ages since I've seen anything green and growing."

"Pining for home already?" he asked, startled. "But you've only been here a few weeks." Most women viewed the country as a place of exile, longing for the gaiety of London whenever they were away.

"It's not the country I miss, but the people. I've never been away from my family before, and I can't help thinking about them. It seems so strange not to be there, not to be part of their lives."

There was a wistful sadness in her expression that made him want to reach over and comfort her. He felt suddenly protective of the naive young miss. He wondered how he would have felt at her age, if he had been sent to London, knowing no one except her aunt. Lady Barton was hardly the type to trouble herself to make her niece feel welcome.

"And yourself? Is your family in London, my lord?" Miss Sedgwick prompted.

"No, my parents are back in Sussex. They prefer the country, and visit London only rarely."

"And your brothers and sisters?"

"None. I'm their only child." A fact which made him

all too eligible, and accounted for his parents' growing determination to marry him off.

"How sad for you!" Miss Sedgwick exclaimed. "I can't imagine life without my brothers and sisters."

"When I was younger I wanted a brother, but my parents presented me with a pony instead. All in all, I believe it was the better bargain."

"There speaks a man with no siblings. Perhaps I should lend you one of mine."

"And do you have enough to spare?"

Miss Sedgwick laughed, her green eyes dancing with mischief. "Assuredly. With four brothers and four sisters, you can have your choice, *Cousin* Matthew."

It was Glendale's turn to blink incredulously. Large families were not unheard-of, but they were not common among the nobility. Eight siblings! If Miss Sedgwick had any sense, she'd be grateful for the relative peace and quiet of London.

A few minutes later, they were hailed by one of Glendale's acquaintances. Glendale had spotted Sir Peter Verney riding in the distance, but hoped the man would have the decency to leave them alone. Instead Verney rode up alongside them, and politeness dictated that they stop to exchange greetings.

"Good afternoon, Glendale. I didn't expect to see you here today." Sir Peter Verney looked speculatively over at Miss Sedgwick. There was something calculating in that gaze, and Glendale hurried to make introductions.

"May I present my cousin, Miss Sedgwick? Miss Sedgwick, this is Sir Peter Verney, an acquaintance of mine." An acquaintance that he would just as soon deny. Sir Peter was in his mid-thirties. A younger son who had never known the weight of responsibility, he had given his life over to idleness and debauchery. But no public scandal had broken, and he was received almost everywhere. The ladies of the *ton* were fond of likening him to a poet, and indeed he had the look of one, with long blond hair, a pallid complexion, and a frame that was thin to the point of emaciation. It was only when you looked closely that you could see the signs of dissipation.

"A pleasure to meet you, sir," Miss Sedgwick replied. She had the poor taste to smile at the cad, as if genuinely pleased to make his acquaintance.

Sir Peter took the gloved hand she offered, raising it to his lips, while looking steadily into her eyes. Dammit, what was the man thinking? Miss Sedgwick wasn't some Covent Garden light-skirt, but a respectable woman. Glendale cleared his throat loudly, and Sir Peter relinquished Miss Sedgwick's hand. He turned his mocking attention towards Glendale.

"Glendale, you dog, I should have known you would steal a march on the rest of us. Where have you been hiding this charmer?" Sir Peter's insinuating smile made it clear that he didn't believe that Miss Sedgwick was Glendale's cousin. Glendale had never liked the man, but up until now he had tolerated him as someone who moved in the same circles. With difficulty, Glendale controlled the urge to plant his fist in the middle of that leering face.

He snapped the reins, making the horses fidget, and unsettling Sir Peter's mount. He took a petty pleasure in watching Sir Peter's attempts to bring his high-strung bay under control.

"I can see your horse is too fresh to be kept standing," Glendale observed. "And Lady Barton is waiting for our return. Good day."

With that, Glendale drove off, leaving an astonished Sir Peter behind. No doubt the man was trying to reconcile the notion of a high-stickler like Lady Barton with his previous assumptions.

"Did I miss something?" Miss Sedgwick asked. "You were very short with your friend."

"He's not my friend. Just an acquaintance. And someone

whom you should stay away from," Glendale growled, still upset by the encounter. What did it matter if he was not in the habit of being seen with eligible young ladies? That didn't give Sir Peter the right to assume that Miss Sedgwick was less than respectable, just because he had taking her out driving.

"Why?"

"Because—" he began, and then hesitated as he tried to think of how to phrase his words. "Because Sir Peter is not the kind of man you ought to know."

"Then why did you introduce me?" pointed out the ever-logical Miss Sedgwick.

"You would have seen him eventually. Sir Peter's received almost everywhere. But he's a rake and a fortune hunter. Just stay away from him, Jane."

"Well, in that case I should be quite safe from his attentions," Jane replied, her voice frosty. "How lucky that I have you to look after my interests."

From the tone of her voice, he knew his abrupt command had offended her. But surely it was better that she learn the truth now. And what had she meant by saying that she was safe? He glanced over, but one look at Jane's set face made him decide against asking her to explain.

Later, in the privacy of her room, Jane attempted to sort out her feelings. *Dear Mama,* Jane began her letter. *I am quite well, and hope that you and the children are the same. London is overwhelming, but everyone is quite kind to me. I have made a new friend, Lord Glendale, who is Lord Barton's nephew. Lord Glendale is as handsome as Rosemarie could wish for, and has all the ladies of the ton at his feet. I miss you and the children dreadfully, and hope that you will write soon, and tell me everything that has happened since I left. And tell Angus MacLeod that I am still waiting to hear how Percival is settling in.*

There now. Jane scanned the beginning of the letter. This was her third attempt. The previous attempts lay crumpled on the floor around her chair, having sounded too much like pleas for sympathy. There was no sense in writing about her troubles. Her family was too far away to help, so why worry them?

If only there was someone that she could confide in. Jane had expected that she would feel uncomfortable at first, but she had been here over three weeks, and had yet to find her feet. She had nothing in common with the other young ladies she met. Even the simplest of things brought the potential for disaster.

Look at the other day. Jane had accompanied Lady Barton while her aunt made her round of calls. Lady Barton had carefully instructed Jane not to talk about politics, her family, or, heaven forbid, trade. The weather had seemed a safe enough topic. So when Mrs. Dunne had commented that the weather was unusually warm for this time of year, Jane felt safe in responding that the weather was warm indeed, which was fortunate with lambing season about to start.

Her cheeks burned as she remembered the wave of laughter that had swept Mrs. Dunne's salon. Mrs. Dunne seemed to feel that Jane had been mocking her, and delivered a stinging lecture on the impertinence of youth. There were only a half dozen people present to witness her embarrassment, but to Jane it seemed like a hundred.

She should go back home. She had nothing in common with these people, and she had no desire to become better acquainted with them. She had no interest in the latest fashions, or discussing the relative merits of one face cream over another, or in listening to scurrilous tales about people she had never met.

Jane thanked heaven that her mother had had the good sense to marry her father. No wonder they had fallen in love. Her father had been a kind man, with a direct, practical way about him. It was impossible to imagine him mingling with the fops and dandies of London.

Of course, not all the men she had met were fops. Matthew Kingsley, for instance. She thought her father would have approved of Lord Glendale. Since their first meeting, she had felt a kinship with him. Jane found herself looking for him wherever she went. His presence livened up the dullest of affairs, while without him all entertainments seemed sadly flat. But for all his seeming enjoyment of her company, Lord Glendale was obviously not in the market for a wife. If only she could find someone else as interesting.

Jane laid down her pen with a sigh. It was time to dress for dinner. She would finish the letter tomorrow. And there was no time to indulge in a fit of the dismals. She was in London for a reason, and she shouldn't let her difficulties make her lose sight of her goal.

True, she was different from the young ladies of the *ton,* but that didn't diminish her worth. Jane might feel out of place here, but girls like Miss Blake would be even more out of place in the country. She'd like to see one of them try to run a household or manage a farm. She chuckled at the idea of the elegant Miss Blake standing shrieking in the middle of a pen, while the sheep pressed around her.

What Jane needed was a man who could appreciate her finer qualities. Someone who would be a friend, as well as a husband. But where would she find such a man? An image of a tall, broad-shouldered man with dark brown hair and laughing brown eyes crossed her mind. Lord Glendale. Drat the man, why was he forever breaking into her thoughts? It wasn't as if he was the only gentleman she knew. She had met dozens of gentlemen since her arrival in town. Not all of them were arrogant fops. Some were kind or clever or even handsome.

But none of them made her feel as special as she did

when she was with Glendale. But was it all in her imagination? She had met Lord Glendale first, so it was natural that she used him as the standard to which she compared all other gentlemen. Surely she could find another gentleman equally worthy of her admiration. Of course she could. It was only a matter of setting her mind to it.

Chapter Five

"Have you finished?" Jane asked for the fifth time in as many minutes.

"Just one more, miss." The maid Sally tucked the ends of the last ribbon securely into Jane's hair. "There now, it's done."

Jane rose from her chair and walked over to the cheval mirror. An elegant stranger peered back at her.

"Oh miss, you look ever so fine," Sally said.

Jane couldn't help agreeing. The reflection in the mirror was she, yet at the same time it was not. The young lady in the mirror was wearing a creamy lace ball gown, over an underskirt of the palest green muslin. Emerald green ribbons decorated the hem and caught up the layers, matching the green and white ribbons that were woven in her hair. The simplicity suited her height, giving her the appearance of elegance and sophistication.

The bodice was square-cut and low. Much too low. Jane started as she realized just how much creamy white bosom was exposed.

"There's been a mistake," Jane said, tugging irritably at the neckline. "This is much too low. I can't possibly be seen like this." There were simply acres of bosom showing.

Sally examined the neckline critically. "It looks fine to me, Miss Jane. But if you'd like, I could tuck in a fichu," she added doubtfully.

Jane examined her reflection again. A fichu wouldn't do the trick. She felt more like wrapping herself in a shawl. She knew she was being irrational. Lady Barton had approved all of her gowns. Surely Lady Barton wouldn't let her appear in anything improper.

"I suppose this is not all that daring," Jane ventured.

"You look lovely. Just the way you ought. Lady Barton will be so pleased."

It was not Lady Barton's opinion that she worried about. What would the gentlemen think? Lord Glendale, for instance. Well, one thing was certain. After seeing her in this dress, Lord Glendale would realize that she was very much of a woman. The thought gave her a shiver of anticipation.

There was just one thing lacking. "Bring me the lacquer box," Jane ordered. Sally obligingly fetched the box. Jane opened it and drew out her mother's necklace. The strand of pearls glistened softly in the lamplight. Jane had not wanted to bring the pearls to London, but her mother had insisted. "My mother gave them to me for my presentation, and now they are yours," Lady Alice had said.

Jane had been touched by the gift, and frightened by the responsibility. What if she lost them? The pearl necklace and earbobs were the only inheritance that her mother had received from her parents. When Lady Alice had defied her family to marry Arthur Sedgwick, a modest landowner, her parents refused to acknowledge the marriage and cut all connection.

Lady Alice remained hopeful that her parents would reconcile themselves to the match over time. She even named her first child Cornelia, after her own mother. But there was no reconciliation. Lord and Lady Wolcott died within a few years of the marriage, still bitter. With no sons, the title went to a distant cousin. Everything that was not entailed was left to "their only true daughter, Letitia, Lady Barton."

In Jane's mind, the pearls were forever tied up with her mother's gay youth, when she had been the toast of London and fell in love with the worthiest of her admirers, Arthur Sedgwick. And although a set of pearls worth several hundred pounds was a luxury they could not afford, Jane had never even considered selling them. Selling the pearls would be like denying her mother's heritage.

Sally fastened the triple strand of pearls around her neck, and Jane had to admit that they added just the right touch. Lady Barton swept into the room just as Jane was preparing to go downstairs.

"Well, now, let me have a look at you," Lady Barton commanded.

Jane stood obediently still.

"I must thank you for your kindness, Lady Barton. This gown is the most wonderful thing I have ever worn," Jane effused.

"Of course it is," Lady Barton said, examining Jane's appearance with a critical air. "Your height is unfortunate, but there must be some gentleman who will be prepared to overlook that defect."

Jane clenched her teeth. Lady Barton was a puzzle that she could not fathom. On the one hand, her sponsorship of Jane was very generous indeed. Jane winced every time she thought of the money that her aunt was spending for this Season, for garments of all descriptions, dancing lessons, and even a coiffeur to style Jane's hair. Not to mention this lavish come-out ball.

It should have been easy for Jane to feel grateful, but it was not. In Lady Barton's hands, each gift was a weapon.

She took every opportunity to remind Jane that these were things that her own family couldn't provide for her. It was as if she was revenging herself on Jane for some past slight.

Lady Barton peered closely at the pearls around her niece's neck. "I see you have my mother's pearls," she said peevishly.

"No," Jane said firmly. "I am wearing my mother's jewelry."

Lady Barton sniffed disdainfully, but forbore to argue. "Well, Cornelia, are you ready? Or do you propose to keep our guests waiting while you wool-gather?"

Lady Barton swept out of the room, and Jane followed, muttering under her breath as she counted to ten for patience. It was going to be a long evening.

But even Lady Barton's criticisms couldn't dampen Jane's enthusiasm for long. Jane knew that she looked her best this evening, and this knowledge gave her the courage to meet the Polite World on equal footing.

Lady Barton had invited a few select guests to partake of dinner before the ball. Although Jane was nominally the reason for the event, the guests tended to ignore her in favor of conversing with each other. This suited Jane just fine. She only needed to converse with her dinner partner, a Mr. James Whitmore.

Mr. Whitmore was an older gentlemen, in his late thirties or early forties. From Lady Barton's introduction, Jane gathered that he was a man of importance in the City, London's financial world. His face was kind, and his manners unassuming. Jane found herself warming to him at once.

"Lady Barton mentioned that you were from Yorkshire?" Mr. Whitmore asked.

"Yes," Jane replied, as the footmen began serving the first course. "My family resides in Barkhamsted. It's just a short distance from York," she added, at his look of incomprehension.

"I visit York on occasion, to check on my investments there. The countryside is beautiful, but wild. London must be quite a change for you."

Why did gentlemen always feel it necessary to comment on the obvious? "It was overwhelming at first, but I am beginning to feel more at home."

"And your parents? Will they be joining you for the Season?"

The question was bland, but behind his polite *facade* Jane sensed a keen intelligence. Mr. Whitmore was wondering why Jane was being sponsored by her aunt, instead of by her mother, as would be the usual case.

"My father has been gone for several years now, and my mother prefers to stay at home with my brothers and sisters." Having no wish to spread the news of her relative poverty, Jane had grown adept at such half-truths.

"My sympathies for your loss. I know that you and your brothers and sisters must be a comfort to your mother," Mr. Whitmore said. He was looking in her direction, but the wistful expression on his face made her realize that he was thinking of something or someone else.

"I am afraid that we are more often a trial than a comfort, but I know that Mama would be desolate without us." Jane paused, taking a sip of the clear soup. "Of course, it is easier now that Michael, the youngest, is out of leading strings. Although I don't know how much of a blessing that is. In her last letter, Mama reported that Michael had taken it in his head to present the Vicar with a large green frog, as a token of the high esteem in which the children hold him."

Mr. Whitmore smiled, and she knew that she had succeeded in luring him out of his brown study. "I was raised in the city myself, but I can imagine no truer gesture of friendship."

"Fortunately Mr. Poole, the vicar, took it in stride. He

has known us forever, and is accustomed to the occasional prank."

"You miss Michael," Mr. Whitmore observed, breaking into Jane's recollections.

"Yes," she said. "And Jonathan. And Ellen. And Bobby and Dick and Emily and Katherine and even Rosemarie."

Mr. Whitmore shot her a look that Jane could not interpret. Had she managed to offend him? Lady Barton had warned her not to talk too much about her family, as it was considered common. But he seemed to be enjoying the conversation.

"I came from a large family myself," Mr. Whitmore said, after a moment's consideration. "My wife and I had hoped for children of our own, but it was not to be."

"I am sorry," Jane said awkwardly. Mr. Whitmore was still in mourning for his wife, who had died earlier in the year. "It must be sad to be so alone."

Mr. Whitmore acknowledged her sympathy, then turned the conversation to less personal topics.

After dinner Jane stood beside her aunt in the receiving line, greeting a seemingly endless stream of visitors. She soon gave up trying to remember them all. The few faces that she did know stood out like welcome beacons. Even Miss Blake received an enthusiastic greeting.

Guests continued to arrive for well over an hour, until Jane felt ready to explode with anticipation. Finally Lady Barton signalled that it was time to enter the ballroom.

Jane caught her breath with wonder. The dusty, unused ballroom had been transformed for the occasion. White trellises draped with garlands of silk flowers gave the illusion of an outdoor fete. The room glittered under the lights of the chandeliers, while the throng below was no less magnificent. The cream of society was here, young ladies in their pale muslins, married ladies in vibrant silk gowns, and gentlemen in the dark colors favored by Beau

Brummel, or the more brilliant plumage of the dandy set. Never could she have imagined such splendor.

Jane's gaze swept the room, wondering how anyone could possibly find anyone else in the confusion. She gave a start when Lord Glendale appeared, as if summoned by her thoughts.

"I believe this is my dance, Miss Sedgwick," Lord Glendale said. He signalled to the musicians, who obediently began to play.

Jane nodded, nervous now that the moment had arrived. She was grateful that Lady Barton had arranged for Glendale to open the ball with her, rather than some stranger. The floor, which had seemed impossibly crowded a moment before, began to clear, as couples formed on the sidelines.

Jane placed her gloved hand on Lord Glendale's, and he led her to the center of the floor. The musicians began to play. Jane froze, unable to remember a single step of the dance. Lord Glendale must have sensed her panic, for he squeezed her hand sympathetically. "Relax," he whispered. "Just pretend that it's only the two of us, and that Mancini is providing the accompaniment." He gave her a conspiratorial grin.

The memory of that lesson made her smile, and she had no difficulty following along as Glendale led her through the first measures. Gradually other couples joined in, until the room was a sea of dancers. Now that she was no longer the center of attention, Jane's nervousness gave way to rising excitement. Tonight was turning out to be everything she had hoped for. The gown that had seemed so daring in her room now made her feel the height of sophistication. For the first time since she had come to London she felt elegant, able to hold her own with any woman in the room.

Lord Glendale smiled at her again, setting her stomach to fluttering. The admiration in his gaze showed that he approved of her transformation. Even through her gloves she could feel the warmth of his hand, and the solidness of his frame that owed nothing to padding. She tilted her head slightly so she could gaze into his eyes, conscious of how Glendale's own height made her feel delicate.

As they twirled through the ballroom, Jane overheard someone saying how well-matched she and Glendale appeared. Their words echoed her feelings precisely. She wished that the music would never end, and that she could go on dancing with Glendale all night.

After the dance was over, Lord Glendale returned Miss Sedgwick to the care of her aunt. For appearances' sake he led out another lady of his acquaintance, a married woman known to be fond of her husband. No risk there. But he was not in the mood for further frolicking, so after helping himself to a glass of champagne, he leaned against a convenient pillar and observed the scene.

There was no reason for him to stay. Miss Sedgwick was doing quite well without his help. Lady Barton introduced Miss Sedgwick to a series of unexceptional gentlemen, making sure she had a partner for each dance. Just now the orchestra was playing a waltz, and Miss Sedgwick was sitting on the side, as befitted a young lady who had not yet received permission for the still controversial dance.

Should he go over there and join her? No, she seemed absorbed with her companion, Mr. James Whitmore. What could the two of them possibly have to talk about? Mr. Whitmore was at least twenty years her senior. A tradesman who had turned the one mill he inherited form his father into a pottery empire, Whitmore was an odd choice for Lady Barton to have invited. Whitmore's fortune made him acceptable to the lower ranks of the *ton,* but that didn't mean that Lady Barton should encourage him to pay attention to Jane.

"Stop scowling. You're frightening the children," Lord Frederick greeted him.

"Hullo, Freddie. I thought you had turned coward, and weren't going to make it this evening."

"And go back on my word? Never," Freddie declaimed. "Besides, I had to see how our rustic miss was faring."

"Observe for yourself, my friend." The orchestra had begun the cotillion, and Glendale saw Miss Sedgwick take the floor with her partner.

"I don't see her," Freddie complained, his eyes sweeping the room.

"There she is." Glendale nodded to indicate the direction. "With Lord David Cartland."

Freddie raised his quizzing glass. "Good lord, you're right. Who would have guessed she'd turn out so pretty?"

Lord Frederick's admission should have pleased Glendale, but it did not. Glendale's concentration was fixed on the couple on the dance floor. Lord David Cartland was an amiable young man, but a full head shorter than Miss Sedgwick. They made an awkward couple, but Lord David didn't seem to mind, fixing his attention on Jane's bosom, instead of on her face.

"You're scowling again," Freddie said, breaking into his thoughts. "If you keep that up, people will think that you are serious about the chit."

"I was not scowling," Glendale said pettishly. "And I am merely looking out for my interests."

Lord Frederick bowed and smiled at a passing acquaintance. "Next time we wager, remind me to be more precise in setting the terms. It won't do at all to have you influencing the outcome."

"What do you mean?"

"Come now, there are no secrets in the *ton*. I heard all about your drive in the park with Miss Sedgwick. Not to mention that you've practically run tame here in the last week, calling every day."

Glendale thought furiously for a moment. "Priscilla! Your sister Priscilla was here the day I called."

"Exactly. I must admit I admire your tactics. People are beginning to talk. They're wondering if you are just doing your duty by a cousin, or if your interest has been truly captured. The speculation will ensure that Miss Sedgwick is a sensation. If I didn't know you better, I'd wonder the same myself."

Lord Frederick was coming too close to matters that Glendale didn't want to think about. "Lady Barton is bearing our way, with Miss Webster in tow. I believe she plans on making you do the pretty," Glendale lied.

"Time to disappear then, before I am forced to stand up with that squint-eyed antidote. You will excuse me," Freddie said, before beating a hasty retreat in the direction of the card room.

Glendale smiled. He had concocted that story on the spur of the moment, but perhaps Lady Barton would be willing to make it true. Miss Webster had been striking terror into the hearts of gentlemen since her debut ten years before. Back then she had been a plain, ill-favored girl, with a disposition to match. Time had not improved either her looks or her temper. She was the despair of hostesses everywhere, who invited her in order to secure the presence of her most eligible brother.

Glendale made his way across the room, intending to drop a word in Lady Barton's ear. Freddie's pointed comments had made him uncomfortable, and it would feel good to pay him back in some measure. Miss Webster ought to be a satisfactory penance.

As he approached the gilt chairs where Lady Barton was holding court, he saw Jane seated next to her aunt. Several gentlemen surrounded the ladies, and Miss Sedgwick glowed under their attentions. Unfortunately Sir Peter Verney was one of their number.

Glendale reached them in time to hear Sir Peter request a dance. "Terribly sorry, but Miss Sedgwick has promised this dance to me," he said blandly.

Miss Sedgwick looked up, her face breaking into a welcoming smile. "Lord Glendale, I have been waiting for you," she said, following his lead. "I was afraid you had forgotten."

"I never forget a promise to a lady," Glendale said, conscious of the eyes that were on them. Taking Miss Sedgwick's hand, he helped her rise. "If you will excuse us, gentlemen, Lady Barton."

He led her to the floor.

"That was quite rude of you, to do that to Sir Peter," Miss Sedgwick said. "But I am glad you did."

At least the chit hadn't forgotten his instructions to stay away from Sir Peter.

"I didn't have a chance to thank you earlier," Miss Sedgwick continued on. "This is the most wonderful night of my life, and I have you to thank for it."

"Me?" Why on earth would she be thanking him?

"Yes. You've been so kind to me. Without your help, I would have been too nervous to enjoy myself. As it is, everyone's been so nice." Miss Sedgwick laughed, her green eyes sparkling with mischief. "Would you believe Lord David Cartland actually called me beautiful?"

Kind. She thought he was being kind. She trusted him as a friend. He felt his heart twist at the thought of that damnable wager. He could only hope that Miss Sedgwick never learned of it. For all her newfound elegance, she suddenly seemed fragile to him. Learning of the wager could destroy her.

"Of course he was only being gallant, but still it was nice to hear," Miss Sedgwick confided.

"Are you saying that you are not beautiful?" Glendale asked gruffly.

"Now that sounds like I am fishing for compliments, my lord. Let us just say that I've seen myself in the glass often enough to know my own looks."

Glendale surveyed her with his gaze. She had taken his

breath away when he first saw her earlier this evening. Jane possessed a regal elegance that far surpassed the dainty beauties of the *ton.* His gaze lingered on the *décolletage* of her gown, which revealed the shape of her firm young breasts. No wonder Lord David had been fascinated. His gaze finally settled on her midnight black hair.

Ribbons were woven through her hair, and he wondered what she would do if he removed the ribbons and let her hair cascade down her back. With an effort of will, he blinked away the image of Jane, covered in nothing but those long tresses, smiling up at him from his bed. What was wrong with him? This was his cousin, not some lady of dubious virtue. He couldn't possibly be attracted to her. He assumed a mask of forced cheerfulness, hoping fervently that none of his lustful thoughts had shown on his face.

"You are right," he said, harkening back to her earlier comment. "You are far too striking to be one of the pale, watery misses the *ton* calls beautiful. Their looks will bloom and fade in a short season, but you will be handsome until the day you die."

"It is kind of you to say so," Jane replied. Her face was suddenly grave, and her eyes searched his, looking for the meaning behind his words.

Now he had really put his foot in it. He had meant to say something conventional, but for once his polished mannerisms had failed him. A less sensible girl than Jane might mistake his words for a declaration.

"I am sure you will hear many more such compliments before the evening is over," Glendale said, trying to lighten the mood. But he was unable to recapture their earlier closeness. It was a relief when the set was finished, and he could return Miss Sedgwick to her aunt.

He made his compliments and then left the ballroom without a backward glance. Miss Sedgwick was disturbing his hard-earned peace of mind. After his faithless fiancée had jilted him, Glendale had sworn that never again would he let his heart rule his head. And yet here he was, letting Jane's sparkling eyes tempt him into uttering words that he had never thought to say. Who knows what else he might do, if he fell under her spell? He had to get away from here, far away, until this fit of madness passed.

Chapter Six

Lord Glendale's partiality did not go unnoticed. The gentlemen flocked to Jane's side, eager to discover what it was that had caught the interest of such a notoriously elusive *parti.*

Jane had her pick of partners for every dance. It was gratifying to be the center of attention, but also fatiguing. Her admirers wouldn't hear of her sitting out a dance. Finally, one of them had the unintentional kindness to trod on the hem of her gown, tearing a flounce. Jane seized the opportunity to escape to the ladies' cloakroom.

"I'll have this fixed in a trice, miss," said the maid Anna, who had already helped two other ladies in similar circumstances.

"Don't hurry on my account," said Jane, sinking gratefully into the chair. "It feels wonderful to be sitting down."

The door opened and Miss Blake entered.

"Good evening, Miss Blake," Jane greeted her. "I pray that you have not suffered a mishap with your gown, as well."

''What? Oh, no, I merely came in here to fix my hair. The pins have been coming loose, and I was afraid they were about to fall out.'' So saying, Miss Blake crossed over to the dressing table and sat in front of the mirror. She then began to fiddle with her elaborately styled hair. There was nothing wrong with it as far as Jane could see, which just went to show how little she knew about such things.

''I hope you are enjoying yourself,'' Jane said, as the silence grew awkward.

''Yes, it is quite marvelous. You must give my compliments to Lady Barton. This has been the event of the Season. Everyone who is anyone is here. And the Marquis of Hawksley was most particular in his attentions.''

''Indeed,'' Jane said, for lack of anything better to say.

''Of course, you must be pleased as well. Everyone is talking about you and Lord Glendale. Is it true that he danced with you twice?''

''Yes,'' Jane said slowly.

''And he left after the second dance. As if he was only interested in you. How thrilling!'' Miss Blake exclaimed, her eyes shining at the prospect of romance.

''It wasn't like that,'' Jane said. ''Lord Glendale is my cousin, after all. He was merely being polite.'' Even as she said the words, she wondered if they were true. The first dance had been duty, but the second? Had he finally noticed her as something more than a mere acquaintance?

''Well, I have several cousins myself, but none of them has ever looked at me the way Glendale looked at you. Still, I suppose you know best.'' On that note, Miss Blake rose and swept out of the room.

Jane sat pondering Miss Blake's remarks. Was Miss Blake being romantic, or were Glendale's attentions something out of the ordinary? For her own part, Jane knew that she was happy when she was with him. But tonight had been much more than that. Tonight he had made her feel as if she were truly a beautiful woman, capable of attracting a man. But the moment had been all too brief, and when he left the magic went out of the evening. Had Glendale felt the same attraction for her that she felt for him? And if so, why had he left in such a hurry?

"There now, that's done it," Anna said, breaking into her thoughts.

"What? Oh, the gown." Jane said, recollecting herself. A quick glance revealed no signs of the maid's skillful repairs. "Thank you, Anna."

A thoughtful Jane returned to the ballroom, where she was once again besieged by her admirers. There was no time to think, and Lord Glendale's unusual behavior was pushed to the back of her mind.

The ball lasted until the small hours of the morning, and the sun was near to rising when Jane finally sought her bed. It was past ten o'clock when she awoke, and for the first time, Jane understood her aunt's fondness for fashionable hours. No wonder the *ton* preferred to sleep late, if such long evenings were their habit.

In the bright light of morning, last night seemed like an impossible dream. Had she really been the belle of the ball? Was it possible that she had danced every dance, turning away potential partners when her dance card was filled?

It seemed too good to be true, yet the evidence was there for all too see. Flowers arrived all morning. Browning, the butler, brought her the cards on a silver tray. Lord This, Sir That, the Honorable John Something, Jane didn't remember being introduced to half the gentlemen who sent tributes. How embarrassing if she should see one of them again, and not be able to thank him!

The flowers were just the beginning. In the afternoon, guests from the previous evening called to pay their respects. Lady Barton had explained that it was the custom for gentlemen who had partnered a young lady to call on her the following day. But her admirers from last evening were not the only ones who came. The ladies of the *ton* arrived as well, with their daughters in tow. Their presence could be put down to excessive politeness, or an innate ability to sense the presence of their quarry, a large gathering of eligible men.

The drawing room was brimming over, but ill luck placed an empty seat next to Jane just as Mrs. Dunne was announced.

"Well, there must be more to you than meets the eye, that's for sure," Mrs. Dunne said, by way of greeting.

"I'm afraid I don't understand," Jane replied.

"Don't play the fool with me, gel." Mrs. Dunne poked Jane in the ribs with the ancient fan that she still carried, a relic of her youth. "Lord Glendale set the cat among the pigeons last night. Now everyone is wondering just what his intentions are."

Jane's heart gave an odd skip. Mrs. Dunne had given voice to her own hidden hopes. Last night had been special, even magical. She felt something for Matthew that she had never felt for anyone before. Did he feel the same way? Or was it too much to hope for?

But Jane had no intention of sharing her new, fragile feelings with anyone. Hoping to cut the conversation short, she replied, "I am sure you are mistaken. Lord Glendale has been very obliging, but only as a favor to our aunt."

"Humph. I've known your aunt for years. Glendale wouldn't go out of his way for her or anyone else. No, if Glendale is doing the pretty, then he has his own reasons."

Mrs. Dunne continued on in the same vein, but Jane refused to be drawn into further conversation. When it became clear that she could not tempt Jane into any indiscretion, Mrs. Dunne switched her attention to another caller who was relating the latest *on-dit.*

Mrs. Dunne wasn't the only trial to bear. The gentlemen

made Jane equally nervous. They all seemed alike, their polished manners hiding their boredom and lack of interest in Jane herself. They presented her with elaborate compliments that left her feeling tongue-tied and awkward.

Jane looked towards the doorway, hoping that Lord Glendale would be among the new arrivals. He wasn't, but she spied James Whitmore, her dinner companion from the last evening. Mr. Whitmore appeared taken aback by the large gathering, pausing for a moment on the threshold before making his way over to her.

"May I offer my congratulations, Miss Sedgwick? It seems you are quite the sensation," Mr. Whitmore said, as he seated himself on the chair that Mrs. Dunne had just vacated.

Jane regarded him with warmth. Mr. Whitmore had seemed a kind, sensible gentleman, and his appearance today only confirmed her good opinion. Unlike the dandies, whose skintight jackets and elaborate cravats bespoke hours of preparation, Mr. Whitmore was dressed in what she could only consider a sensible style. Eschewing the extremes of fashion, Mr. Whitmore's clothes were designed for comfort as well as appearance. In many ways, he reminded Jane of her late father.

"How very kind of you to call today," Jane replied. "I am sure you have more important errands you could be about."

"I was glad to come, although it appears that you wouldn't have noticed my absence." Whitmore gestured to the crowded room, and smiled deprecatingly.

"Oh, these fribbles," Jane said dismissively. "They have decided to declare me a sensation, and have come to pay their court. But such men are notoriously fickle, and no doubt they will soon find another lady who captures their fancy." As flattering as the attention was, she was too honest to pretend that it would last.

"That's a very practical attitude," he said consideringly.

Practical. Jane stifled a pang of disappointment. Hadn't she been telling herself how tired she was of empty compliments? She should welcome Mr. Whitmore's plain-speaking.

Mr. Whitmore continued on. "You said last evening that you haven't had an opportunity to see much of London. I would be happy to escort you, with Lady Barton's permission, of course."

"I would be delighted," Jane said, with her first real enthusiasm of the morning. It would not be the same as seeing the town with Lord Glendale, but Matthew had yet to offer and she wouldn't presume upon his kindness to beg for an invitation.

They agreed that the excursion should take place two days hence. Mr. Whitmore kept up an easy flow of conversation for the remainder of his half hour. Before leaving, he remembered to secure Lady Barton's approval for the excursion.

It was kind of Mr. Whitmore to have called. Outside of Lord Glendale, he was the only one of her new acquaintances that she enjoyed speaking with. Which was strange, since her feelings for the two men were so dissimilar. Mr. Whitmore, with his plain ways and sensible conversation, was very much like the uncle she had always wished to have.

Her feelings for Lord Glendale were entirely different. She had grown used to thinking of him as a friend, but there had been something warmer than mere friendship between them last night. She had felt it. She could have sworn that he felt the attraction, too. Yet where was he? Why was he the only one of her admirers who stayed away?

Lord Glendale did not see Miss Sedgwick until a week had passed since the ball. It wasn't for lack of trying on his part. Miss Sedgwick's newfound popularity meant that he had been reduced to sending an invitation ahead of time, to ensure that she would be free.

"Good afternoon, my lord," Browning greeted Lord Glendale. "Miss Sedgwick will be down presently. Would you care to wait in the morning room?"

Browning extended his hand, ready to receive Glendale's hat and gloves. Glendale had been prepared to wait, but now he changed his mind. He had no intention of kicking his heels while Miss Sedgwick dallied over her toilette.

"No," he said curtly. "Tell Miss Sedgwick to hurry. There's no sense in keeping the horses standing."

Browning nodded gravely, and motioned to one of the hovering footmen. The message was duly conveyed to Miss Sedgwick. The butler disappeared on some mysterious errand of his own, leaving Glendale alone in the hall.

"Matthew, what a pleasure to see you," Miss Jane Sedgwick said, as she descended the stairs a few moments later.

"Miss Sedgwick. I am honored that you accepted my invitation. I wasn't sure if you would be able to find time for me, with so many other admirers." Even to his own ears, his words sounded churlish.

No sooner had he spoke than he regretted his words. Jane's welcoming smile dimmed, and she looked at him anxiously, as if wondering what wrong she had committed. There was no sense in taking out his ill temper on the girl. It was not Jane's fault that her innocent happiness reproached him. He kept thinking about that damnable wager. If he were truly a gentleman, he would call the whole thing off. But then if he did, he would have no excuse to see her again.

He couldn't think of how to apologize without laying bare the whole tangled coil. Instead he contented himself with helping Jane don her cloak. Escorting her to the waiting carriage, he helped her up, and then took the reins from the waiting groom.

Jane was the first to break the silence. "Lord Glendale, I must thank you for your kindness to me," she said stiffly. "The ball was all that Lady Barton had hoped for. Whatever modest success I may have this Season, I will owe to you."

The sudden formality hurt. Glendale glanced sideways at his companion. Jane stared straight ahead, refusing to look at him. He was in her black books indeed.

"Miss Sedgwick," he began. "Jane. Forgive my earlier rudeness. I've been in a temper all day, but that doesn't excuse my taking it out on you."

It was a poor excuse, but fortunately Jane seemed prepared to accept it. He could hardly tell her the truth. He didn't even know what the truth was himself.

The wager with Freddie was all but won. His own efforts had seen to that. He should have been pleased with Miss Sedgwick's success. But instead all he felt was an overwhelming irritation. Why should he care if Miss Sedgwick no longer had time for him? It wasn't as if he was really courting the girl.

He had even thought of canceling the wager. After all, it was not the done thing, to make a wager involving an innocent young lady. Glendale knew that Freddie would have no objections. Freddie, despite his initial disdain, had grown to appreciate Miss Sedgwick.

But if he canceled the wager, then he would have no excuse to see her again. And he wasn't ready to do that. It was ironic. The more he wanted to be with Miss Sedgwick, the less time she seemed to have for him. He missed their former easy camaraderie.

The day after the ball, he had walked over to Berkeley Square, intending to call on Jane. But the line of carriages outside his uncle's town house had quickly changed his mind. Glendale had no intention of being just another face in the crowd.

And yesterday, he and Freddie had stopped to pay their respects. Lady Barton had been pleased to see them, but

Miss Sedgwick was nowhere to be seen. Out driving with one of her admirers, Lady Barton had said, with a hint of malice.

"I was so sorry that I missed you yesterday when you called," Jane said, unknowingly echoing his thoughts.

"Don't be," he said, attempting to dismiss the incident as beneath his notice. "Lady Barton mentioned that you were out for a drive?"

"Yes. It has been so busy, that I haven't had any time to see anything. Outside of the modiste and the shops, that is. When Mr. Whitmore offered to show me around London, I jumped at his offer."

Mr. Whitmore again. That fellow seemed to turn up everywhere. He should have a talk with Lady Barton about the propriety of allowing such an ineligible prospect to monopolize Jane's time. Mr. Whitmore might be wealthy, but he was not really a gentleman. Jane could do much better than a middle-aged Cit.

"And did you enjoy yourself?" he couldn't help asking.

"It was marvelous!" Jane replied, her eyes shining in remembrance. "He wanted to take me to the Royal Museum and the Tower, but I persuaded him to take me to the Guild Hall and the 'Change instead."

"The Guildhall?" he asked, in disbelief.

"You know, the old wool merchants' guild," Jane said, a trifle impatiently. Enthusiasm gave her green eyes a sparkle, and imparted an enchanting liveliness to her countenance. If only he were the cause of her enthusiasm, he thought, and then wondered why it should matter to him.

But his silence went unnoticed. "Years ago it used to be a real guild, of course, but now it is just the capital of the wool traders. Mr. Whitmore knows simply everyone. He took me in, and introduced me to the senior partners. And everyone was so helpful," she concluded.

Glendale glanced over at the blissfully happy Miss Sedgwick. Had he gone mad or had she? "He took you to the City?"

His disapproval must have been plain. "Don't be so stodgy," Jane said, poking him playfully in the side. "It was perfectly proper. And it would be a shame if I had missed this opportunity. I even found someone who will act as my agent, and market the wool from our new cross-breeds, once we have the first shearing."

Miss Sedgwick's enthusiasm was plain to see. But there was no sense in encouraging this latest mad start. "Mr. Whitmore did not do you any favors," he countered. "If word of this expedition gets out, it could ruin your reputation."

Jane gave him a scornful look. "Fiddlesticks! There was nothing improper in what we did. He wouldn't even take me into the 'Change. Said no ladies were allowed. But he did drive by and point it out to me, along with the coffeehouses where he says the real business is done."

"A proper young lady wouldn't be interested in such things," Glendale said, reduced to falling back on platitudes. "It isn't seemly for you to concern yourself with trade."

"Well, they had better concern themselves with money, or all those young ladies will find themselves in the gutter," Jane said cuttingly.

"That's not the point," Glendale replied. He wasn't sure what the point was, except that Jane seemed to prefer the company of a middle-aged bore over his own.

Jane said nothing, merely arching a delicate eyebrow to indicate her disbelief.

"Trading is best left to men like Mr. Whitmore. In his own way he's worthy enough, I suppose, solidly middle-class and respectable. But he's a merchant, and he'll always be a merchant. His only hope is to marry a lady of the *ton*, and hope that her breeding will compensate for his lack."

"That's a terrible thing to say," Jane leapt to the defense

of the absent Whitmore. "He's worked hard and made something of himself. Why Mr. Whitmore is worth a dozen of those useless dandies that the *ton* prizes so much."

Glendale privately agreed with her, and wondered what had caused him to belittle Mr. Whitmore. It wasn't as if he held a grudge against the man.

"Tell me, where does your income come from?" she challenged.

"What do you mean?"

"This," she said, gesturing to include the curricle and his prime cattle. "Your clothes, your town house, the horses, and gambling, and whatever it is you gentlemen find to spend your blunt on."

He felt himself sinking deeper into a quagmire, and with difficulty controlled the urge to shake some sense into the contrary miss. "I hardly think that is any concern of yours."

"Isn't it? It's the first thing that the chaperones tell their charges. 'Yes, dear, Lord This is quite handsome, but he hasn't a feather to fly with,' or 'Pay attention to Mr. X, he may be a trifle gauche, but he has ten thousand a year, and the prospects of more.' At least I am honest about my interest in trade."

Glendale shifted uncomfortably in his seat. Society was, after all, a very small world. Everyone knew everyone else's affairs as a matter of course. Some gentlemen would speculate about the size of a girl's dowry as readily as they would about her virtue, or lack thereof. It was the way things were done, and he had never before thought to question it. But Jane accepted nothing at face value, and through her he was seeing things in a whole new light.

The appearance of Lord Frederick put an end to the uncomfortable discussion. Freddie rode with them on their final turn around the park. His cheerfulness was impossible to resist, and soon Jane was back in charity with the world.

Careful to avoid the touchy subjects of trade or the attentions of Mr. Whitmore, they chatted about inconsequentials as he drove towards Lady Barton's town house. Glendale went along with the change of topic, but made a mental note to speak to Lady Barton about discouraging Mr. Whitmore.

As they turned into Berkeley Square, Jane startled him by suddenly clutching his sleeve. "Oh no," she said, "It can't be. It mustn't be."

His pulse racing, Glendale yanked on the reins, pulling the carriage to an abrupt halt in front of the Bartons' town house. The horses complained at the unkind treatment, but he was too concerned about Jane to worry.

Glendale looked around, but he could see nothing that would cause Jane's distress. The brownstone town house looked the same as it always did, imposing and inhospitable. The only person in sight was a housemaid, energetically scrubbing down the stone steps.

"What is it?"

Jane lifted her head from where she had buried it against his sleeve. "I cannot bear to look."

Her expression reflected exasperation rather than fright. A semblance of calmness returned to his own thoughts.

"Jane, you're being foolish. Is there something wrong?"

Jane nodded her head in the direction of the square. "Do you see two boys there?" she asked.

"Yes."

"Are they both dark-haired lads, about twelve?"

Glendale looked at the boys closely. The two ragged urchins were certainly out of place in Berkeley Square, but that didn't explain Jane's reaction. The boys had been engaged in some obscure game, but sensing his regard they stood up and returned his stare.

"Yes," he said slowly.

"I knew it was too good to last," Jane said obscurely. "Excuse me, Lord Glendale." She turned away from him, and gave her hand to the groom who had been patiently waiting to help her alight. Stepping down on the pavement, she walked around to the front of the carriage, and called out. "Bobby! Dick! Come over here at once."

The boys waved, and then began making their way across the square.

"May I take it that you are acquainted with the boys?" Glendale asked.

"Yes," Jane sighed. "Those, my lord, are my brothers."

Chapter Seven

The twins waved in response to her call. Jane checked her first impulse to run to them, and instead stood waiting for them to make their own way. Her heart raced and she imagined all sorts of disasters that could have occasioned their presence in London.

The twins ran to her, but halted a few paces away, as if unsure of their welcome. Their eyes flicked nervously to the figure of Glendale, who remained in his carriage, an apparently fascinated spectator.

"Bobby, Dick. What on earth are you doing here?" Jane demanded.

"We had to come," Dick said, then ducked his head and shuffled his feet. She looked at Bobby, but he, too, lowered his eyes. Close up she could see they looked rather the worse for wear. Travel grime stained their clothes and faces. Dick had torn the knees of his breeches, and Bobby had managed to lose his cap.

Jane crossed the remaining few steps and hugged them both. "It is good to see you," she said, ruffling Bobby's hair. "But what are you doing outside? Why didn't you wait for me inside?"

"They didn't believe us when we said we was your brothers."

Bobby nodded in vigorous agreement. "And a pompous old windbag came out and said we were to shove off, before he called the watch."

Browning. Only the self-important butler would have been so callous. True, at the moment her brothers bore more resemblance to street urchins than to the grandsons of a duke, but Browning should have known better. What harm would it have done to let the boys wait inside till she returned to confirm their identities?

"We will just see about that," Jane promised. "Come inside now, and tell me what the trouble is." Gathering up her skirts, she prepared to shepherd them up the steps of the town house.

Glendale waited at the bottom of the steps. She had been too wrapped up with the boys to notice his stepping down from the carriage. He had purposefully chosen a spot that blocked their path. Couldn't he see the awkwardness of her situation? A real gentleman would have left by now. But there was no hope for it, so she made the necessary introductions.

"Lord Glendale, may I present my brothers, Richard and Robert Sedgwick."

Dick dragged off his cap, and the boys executed credible bows.

"Honored to make your acquaintances," Glendale said, solemnly shaking their hands.

"Lord Glendale," she said stiffly, "I thank you for the drive, but as you can see, I have other concerns. I am sure you will excuse me." The last thing she needed was an interloper at this family gathering.

She attempted to step around him, but Glendale would not be budged. "On the contrary," he said, smoothly taking her arm, and escorting her up the stairs. "You promised me tea, after all. And I look forward to the opportunity to become better acquainted with your brothers."

The door was opened by the imperious Browning, putting an end to further debate. The butler's eyes widened as he caught sight of the boys.

"Browning," Jane said haughtily, in her best imitation of Lady Barton. "As you can see, my brothers have arrived from Yorkshire. Have the maids make up a room for them. And see that tea is served directly, in the sitting room."

Browning opened his mouth to protest, and then his gaze settled on the imposing figure of Lord Glendale, entering behind her. "Yes, miss," he said woodenly. "But Lady Barton won't like it."

"I hardly think it your place to pass judgment on Lady Barton's likes or dislikes," Jane said mildly. Browning's face reddened, embarrassed at having been caught in such a presumptuous act.

Glendale assisted Jane in taking off her cloak, then removed his own and handed it to the waiting footman. Following his example, the boys cheerfully shrugged off their own jackets and tossed them in the direction of Browning, who received them with a visible wince.

The boys gazed in wonder at the splendid surroundings, but managed to contain themselves until they reached the sitting room. Jane breathed a sigh of relief to find it unoccupied. Lady Barton preferred the parlor in the afternoons, which was why Jane had chosen the smaller sitting room. Lady Barton would no doubt be informed of their arrival. But if she had callers she would be reluctant to leave them, thus delaying the inevitable confrontation.

"Dick, Bobby, sit on the bench by the fire," Jane ordered, directing them to the one piece of furniture in the room that was not covered with expensive brocades.

Dick settled himself down with a bounce. Bobby followed more slowly, taking time to place his knapsack on the floor.

"Gosh, Jane, don't you look swell. We weren't sure it was you till you waved," Dick said admiringly.

"Thank you, I think," Jane said wryly.

"You look real fine. Rosemarie would scratch your eyes out if she saw you now," Bobby concurred.

Jane winced. So much for small talk. "Does Mama know that you are here?" she asked.

"Yes . . . No," the twins said in unison. They shot each other accusatory looks.

"Which is it?" Jane insisted.

"No."

"Yes."

"What I mean is, that we told her—"

"We didn't exactly tell her—"

"Well, you said not to—"

"No, I said we should and you said—"

The squabbling was interrupted by the arrival of the tea cart. Out of the corner of her eye, Jane saw Dick take advantage of the distraction to kick Bobby in the ankle.

Jane dismissed the hovering maid and served the tea herself, then watched fascinated as the boys piled their plates full of delicacies. Their appetites reassured her. Surely there was nothing seriously wrong at home, if they could eat so unconcernedly.

"Cripes, do you eat like this every day?" Bobby asked, holding a cream scone in one hand and a biscuit in the other. Hunger had apparently won out over good manners.

"Of course she doesn't silly, or she'd be as fat as Mrs. Norton," Dick retorted.

Jane fought the urge to bury her face in her hands. She longed to remind her brothers to mind their manners, but refused to embarrass them by correcting them in front of Lord Glendale.

She looked over towards Glendale, who had been staring at the scene with all the fascination of a man gazing at a menagerie. With no younger siblings or nephews, it was probably years since he had last seen twelve-year-old boys at their mealtime.

"May I take it that these truants have escaped from school?" he enquired.

It was a reasonable deduction, given their ages. And most fashionable schools were close to London.

Bobby shook his head vigorously, then swallowed. "No, sir. We came from home."

"From Barkhamsted. That's in Yorkshire," Dick added helpfully.

"Yorkshire!" Glendale exclaimed. "How on earth did you manage to get here?"

"Andy Turner gave us a ride to York—" Dick began.

"But we had to walk to Collinsville—" Bobby interjected.

"Enough," Jane said. It would take them forever to tell their story in their own way. "Which one of you is Arthur today?"

"I am," Dick said.

"Who is Arthur?" Glendale demanded.

Jane bit back a giggle at his expression. The poor man was at sea. He should leave now while he still had all his wits about him.

"Arthur was my father's name," she explained. "My parents planned on naming the oldest boy Arthur as well."

"But then they had us," Bobby broke in. "And they sorta mixed us up. So no one knows which one is oldest."

"So we take turns being the oldest. 'Cause that's only fair."

Glendale looked aghast, as only a scion of an ancient titled family could. Jane understood his confusion. Growing up she had never questioned her parents' decision that the twins should share everything equally. And the tale of an accidental mix-up had always rung slightly false to her. But now, having been exposed to the nobility, where order of birth was everything, she could see how Glendale would take a dim view of such a casual attitude.

"They mixed you up?" he said faintly.

"Enough," Jane said impatiently. "Dick, you explain what has brought you here. And if he leaves anything out, you can tell us, Bobby. *After* your brother finishes."

Dick took a deep breath and looked down at the floor, nervous now that the moment had come.

"We knew you'd be mad at us, but we had to come." He looked up at her, begging her understanding. "Mama said we weren't to worry you, but we knew you would want to know."

"Know what?"

"Percival George's dead."

Jane froze, her heart constricting in her chest. Her hand shook, rattling the cup in its saucer. She could feel Glendale's gaze on her. Carefully she lowered the cup to the table before her, using the moment to calm herself.

"How did it happen?" she asked, with a valiant attempt at composure.

"Some kind of influenza, Angus said. Squire Jones had it first on his place, and then Percival got sick. Most of the others are fine, though," Dick added reassuringly.

"It was after the Bennetts moved out of the Hall. Folks were mad because they just up and left, and now they owe everyone money," Bobby chimed in, tired of sitting silently.

Jane struggled to bring her thoughts under control. This was beyond belief. She had feared the loss of the tenants, or a setback with the flock, but never in her worst nightmares had she imagined that both would strike at once.

"So you decided to come here? Couldn't you have written a letter instead?" she asked, for lack of anything better to say.

"Mama said we weren't to worry you. Said you had enough on your mind, what with being with Lady Barton and all," Dick replied.

"And we asked Angus, and he agreed with us, but when

Mama said 'No,' he wouldn't go against her," Bobby cut in.

"So we left Mama a note and came," Dick finished up.

"Just like that?" she asked faintly.

"Well, we walked as far as Collinsville, and then Andy Turner gave us a ride in his cart to York. We had our pocket money, but it wasn't enough for the stage."

Jane made a vow to have strong words with Andy Turner when she returned home. Imagine the brains of the man, taking two young boys to York! He had to know they were runaways.

"But then Bobby found Mr. Bender, who was driving a wagon of cloth to London. He said we could ride in the back, if we gave him our coins, and helped him when he reached London. So we did. He even told us how to get to Berkeley Square."

"And we only got lost once or twice," Bobby added.

They had been lucky. Jane tried not to think of all the perils that could have befallen two innocent boys on their own.

"Thank God you made it here safely," Jane said. "And I am grateful that you told me about Percival." Her apparent calmness deceived the boys, who relaxed now that their message was delivered. "But you are still in deep trouble," she continued. "I can't begin to think of what Mama is going through right now, wondering if anything has befallen you. How could you do this to her?"

Dick had the grace to look ashamed, but Bobby merely looked belligerent. "But we had to come," Bobby repeated.

It was too much to absorb all at once. Her apparent calmness was fooling the boys. But Jane feared that Glendale would see through her deception, and sense her inner turmoil. Her heart was beating so loudly that she was sure he could hear it. She needed to bring this gathering to an ending, before she revealed too much.

Seeing that the boys had finally finished demolishing everything on the tea tray, Jane rang the bell. "We'll finish this conversation later," she promised. "Annie, kindly show my brothers up to their room, where they can wash up. I will be up to see you later."

The boys jumped up, eager to be out from under the shadow of her disapproval. Remembering their manners, they made their bows to Glendale. "Honored to have met you, sir," they said in unison, before following the maid out the door.

Jane sank back wearily, exhausted by the effort of maintaining her composure in front of an audience. And the battle had just begun. There was Lady Barton, who would no doubt be furious over her unexpected guests. Jane needed to make arrangements for their swift return.

"Who is Percival George?" Glendale asked, breaking into her train of thought. "Is that another one of your brothers?"

"What? Oh, no, no," Jane said, but refused to elaborate. She didn't feel up to explaining that Percival George Black was a sheep. A very important ram, to be sure, one whom they had hoped would be the foundation of their new flock. But there was no way to explain to Glendale why Percival was so important, without laying bare the whole of their financial condition.

She looked at Glendale, but the sympathy in his eyes was too much to bear. He must think her family a ramshackle lot, after this latest escapade. If only she could confide in him. But from the prickling behind her eyes, she knew she was close to tears. If she began to unburden herself, she would weep. And he would no doubt despise her for a silly female.

The silence stretched, while she thought furiously. What was she to do now? Where would she begin? Could the boys have been exaggerating the extent of the trouble?

Glendale broke into her thoughts. "You look troubled. Is there anything I can do to help?"

Jane was about to refuse when a thought struck her. "Matthew," she asked. "How does one go about buying tickets for the mail coach? Lady Barton will not be pleased to find my brothers here. And Mama is undoubtedly worried sick about them. I think it best if I send them home as soon as possible."

Getting the boys home was the least of her worries, but it was the only one she could share with him. She could feel her heart growing heavier as the full scope of the disaster began to sink in.

"Let me make the necessary arrangements," Glendale offered.

"Oh, no, I couldn't impose," Jane protested, for politeness' sake.

"Nonsense. It is no trouble. My secretary Stapleton is a paragon of efficiency. He'll know just what has to be done. And he's forever complaining that I lead such a quiet life that he has nothing to do."

His self-mocking tone brought a smile to her lips. "Thank you," Jane said, touched by his kindness.

"My privilege to be of service," Glendale said, rising. "And I can see that you have other things on your mind, so I will leave you now. It has been a pleasure, Miss Sedgwick." He paused for a moment on the threshold. "Oh, and don't be too hard on your brothers. They seem like good sorts."

Glendale was in a thoughtful mood as he returned to his town house. It had been a most unusual afternoon. First there had been that strange tension between himself and Jane. And just when it seemed that they were about to get back on their easy footing, the arrival of her brothers had broken the mood.

And what exactly was the meaning of their presence in London? Their visit was no schoolboy prank. The twins had traveled the breadth of the country to find their sister. It was either the most harebrained stunt in creation, or a sign of a disaster of unimaginable proportions.

He had joined her and the boys for tea, in hopes that his presence would deflect Lady Barton's wrath. And although Lady Barton hadn't appeared, he had remained, impelled by his own curiosity. But instead of answers he found only more questions. The boys acted freely enough in his presence. And, if their appetites were any sign, they had no pressing troubles.

But something in their tale had distressed Jane, causing her hands to shake, and her face to go pale. She recovered herself quickly, but after knowing her for these last weeks, Glendale was able to see the signs of strain that others would have missed. What was it in the boys' story that troubled her so? Was it the death of this Percival, whoever he was? Could he be a country swain, left behind as she entered the fashionable world?

The thought of a Jane with her country lover disturbed him. He attempted to reassure himself that her reactions were not those of a grieving woman. No, it was something else that had haunted her eyes.

She looked so helpless that he longed to enfold her in his arms, and promise her that he would make everything all right. The impulse had shocked him, as no doubt the gesture would have shocked her. Instead he offered her the more conventional comfort of his assistance.

He expected his offer to be refused, having learned that Jane treasured her independence. Her acceptance was just another sign that something was severely awry.

His thoughts chased themselves around until his brain was weary with suppositions. Enough. There was no point in speculating until he had more information. But how could he find out more? Jane had made no attempt to confide in him. Her brothers could tell him more, but he could think of no excuse to get them alone. Or could he?

When he reached his town house, the first thing he did was seek out his loyal secretary. "Stapleton. Just the man I wanted to see," Glendale said, striding into his secretary's office.

Stapleton rose from his chair. If his employer's enthusiastic greeting startled him, he gave no sign.

"How may I serve you?" Stapleton asked calmly.

"Sit, sit," Glendale said, perching on a corner of the desk, as Stapleton resumed his seat. Glendale peered at his secretary closely before continuing. "You're looking fatigued, Stapleton. I work you too hard. I think a rest is in order. Yes, some time in the country is just what you need."

"My lord?"

"You're going to Barkhamsted. That's in Yorkshire," Glendale said helpfully. He stood up and began to pace, too restless to sit still. He grinned as he glanced over at his unflappable secretary. If anyone could find out what was going on, Stapleton could.

"And what will I be doing in Yorkshire?"

"Miss Sedgwick's two brothers have paid an unexpected visit to London. They need to be returned home at once."

"And you want me to go with them to ensure that they do not take any unauthorized side trips?" Stapleton surmised.

"Not exactly. Although that is the excuse I'll give, should Miss Sedgwick ask any questions. I want you to keep your eyes and ears open. This jaunt to London was more than a lark. There's something fishy about this whole business. Something is troubling Jane and I want to know what it is." Glendale winced as he realized he had used Jane's given name.

"I see," Stapleton said, with a complete lack of expression. "I am to go to Yorkshire, and see what I can find out."

Sudden doubts assailed him. Was he overreacting? He could be making a fuss over nothing. But his instincts told him otherwise.

"Exactly. I don't know if there is anything there or not, but if there is, I know you will find it out."

"Your confidence in me is appreciated, my lord. When would you like us to leave?"

"Tomorrow's too soon, but Lady Barton is sure to kick up the dust over the boys being here at all. Make the arrangements for Friday, the day after tomorrow. Let me know when everything is ready, and I'll inform Jane, er—Miss Sedgwick."

"Very good, my lord. Is there anything else?"

"No, that's all," Glendale said with satisfaction. He could trust Stapleton to accomplish the job. If there was anything there, he would find it. And in a short time, Glendale would have the key to the mystery of Miss Jane Sedgwick.

Chapter Eight

Jane opened her eyes as the first rays of dawn crept across her windowsill. The morning light signalled an end to the longest night of her life, and it was with relief that she rose from her bed, anxious to begin the day. Her troubles had weighed heavily on her mind all evening, causing her to lie awake for hours. Even when she slept, it was in fitful starts, wakening time and time again from some half-remembered nightmare.

But now it was time for action. Unwilling to wait a moment longer, Jane crossed to the wardrobe and pulled out the first gown that met her eye. She dressed herself quickly, fretting over the tiny buttons that Sally managed with such ease.

Jane sat at the dressing table, brushing her hair. She peered forward at her reflection in the glass. Did the sleepless night show? No, the face that peered back at her was the same as always. A stranger might think her without a care in the world.

As Jane continued brushing, her mind turned back to

the recriminations that had kept her awake. This disaster was all her fault. She should have seen it coming, and made preparations. They should never have mortgaged the Hall. But the mortgage had been the only way to pay off their debts, she reminded herself.

Then she should never have rented out the Hall to strangers, even if it was the only way to pay off the mortgage. Although how could she have known that the tenants would prove untrustworthy? The Bennetts had come highly recommended.

Jane twisted her hair into a knot, then pinned it up. Bending down, she checked her reflection in the glass. No, she thought, it wasn't the tenants who were the problem. They could have ridden out this storm if they hadn't spent their savings on Percival George.

Be honest, she scolded herself. The reason for her anger wasn't the mortgage, the tenants, or even the hapless Percival. She was angry at herself. In the past weeks she had let herself get caught up in the giddy whirl of the London Season, and the pleasure of Lord Glendale's company. She had completely lost sight of the reason for her visit. She, who had always prided herself on her good sense, was as foolish as Rosemarie.

Well, no more, Jane vowed silently. She had come to London to find a husband, and by heaven she would. No more wasting time with dandies who were only interested in a harmless flirtation. From now on she would confine her attentions to gentlemen who were serious in their intentions.

But who among her many admirers could she turn to? There was not one among them that she could think of who would be willing to offer her marriage. Lord David Cartland? No. Lord David was amusing, but she had seen no sign that he regarded her with any special warmth. And with his expectations he could look far higher than the penniless granddaughter of a duke for his bride. Perhaps

Mr. Conard would do. He might be willing, but then again his propensity for gambling was well known. She needed a husband who could help her, not plunge them further into debt.

Jane cast her mind over the gentlemen who had squired her about the past weeks, but for some reason she could not imagine sharing her life with any of them. The image of Lord Glendale flashed through her mind. It was his fault, she decided. His attentions had been so flattering that they left her no time to think of anything else. He had flirted with her and paid her compliments and shown a flattering desire to be in her company. With Matthew she felt that she could be herself, yet at the same time he made her feel as if she was a beautiful and desirable woman. It was enough to turn any girl's head.

If only he had ever shown any sign that he regarded their relationship as more than a harmless flirtation. But she might as well wish for the moon and the stars, as for Lord Glendale to come up to scratch.

Even before her family's impoverishment, it would have been an unequal match. And she had little faith that her own attractions would prove irresistible. How could she hope to capture Matthew's heart, when so many other women had failed to do so? Perhaps if she had had more time, things might have been different. But there was no time, and the dreams that she had cherished to herself would have to be forsaken. It was time that she stopped dreaming, and resigned herself to a marriage of convenience.

Thus resolved, she made her way down the corridor to the room where the boys were staying. She tapped lightly at the paneled door.

"Bobby, Dick, are you awake?" Jane called.

She heard a rustling sound, and Bobby opened the door. "Morning, Jane. We've been waiting for you," he said, busily tucking his shirttail into his breeches.

"And we're starving," Dick added.

Jane surveyed her brothers. She would have to do something about their clothing. Someone had brushed their jackets and mended the tears, but they would never be more than barely presentable. And of course extra clothes hadn't been among the items the boys thought necessary for the journey.

"Come with me then, and we'll see about breakfast." The boys clumped into the hall, their boots making an unholy racket on the polished floor. "Be quiet," she cautioned. "We don't want to wake Lady Barton."

The twins nodded in agreement, and began tiptoeing down the hall with elaborate caution. Their meeting last night with Lady Barton had been an unpleasant experience for all concerned. Only Jane's repeated promise that the boys would return home to Barkhamsted immediately had preserved the peace.

The servants had finally resigned themselves to her habit of rising early, so even at this hour the sideboard in the breakfast room was filled with a variety of breakfast dishes. The twins dug into their food with the enthusiasm that only growing boys can muster. Jane had little appetite, contenting herself with a cup of chocolate and a roll.

"What are we going to do today?" Dick asked, around a mouthful of toast.

Jane had made her plans during the long sleepless night, so was able to reply without hesitation. "I have some errands to run, and you will be coming with me."

"Capital!" Dick exclaimed.

"This is not a reward," Jane said reprovingly. "You are still in disgrace. But I promised Lady Barton that I wouldn't let you out of my sight, so there's no help for it."

The twins refused to be quashed. "Mama will punish us anyway. So as long as we're here, we might as well enjoy it," Bbby said cheerfully.

Jane shook her head ruefully, helpless in the face of twelve-year-old logic.

Two hours later, she was wishing that she had left the boys back at the Hall, and risked Lady Barton's wrath. The twins were bundles of inexhaustible energy. Everything about London excited their interest. They scornfully dismissed the carriage as old-fashioned, but that didn't prevent them from trying to hang their heads out the windows, to ensure that they didn't miss anything.

She took them first to Goodwin's Dry Goods Emporium, to purchase ready-made clothes for the trip home. True to their word, the boys never left her side. But the lure of the shop, with its counters displaying every imaginable type of merchandise, proved a powerful temptation. They dragged her first one way then another, as the brightly colored goods caught their fancy.

Next, she had the coachmen drive them to Bond Street. The coachman let them down at the end of the street, and Jane instructed him to return in an hour. With one hand firmly on the package in her cloak pocket, she led the boys to their destination.

"Here it is," Jane announced.

"We can wait for you outside," Dick offered, after a quick glance at Francesca's plate glass window with its display of bonnets and hats for every occasion.

"We promise we won't go anywhere." Bobby said, nodding vigorously in agreement.

Jane had anticipated their reactions when she planned this morning's itinerary. "No, I think you had better come in with me. This may take a while, and I wouldn't want you to get into any mischief."

The boys looked so crestfallen that she forbore to tease them any longer. "Very well," she said, "Do you see the green sign that says Rawlings' Circulating Library?" Jane indicated a small shop that was three doors down.

"I see it!" Bobby crowed.

She fixed them with a stern look. "You may wait for me in there. But only if you promise not to cause trouble, and not to leave until I come fetch you."

The twins promised, relieved by their narrow escape. Jane watched them until they entered the library. Then she turned and walked into Francesca's. The young woman at the counter betrayed no surprise when Jane returned the bonnet for refurbishing. "I know I asked for the trimmings to be primrose, but it looks simply frightful with my gown," Jane explained. "Please have this redone in scarlet instead, and sent over to Lady Barton's."

The assistant accepted the explanation, and promised to have it ready in a few days. Her ostensible reason for the trip satisfied, Jane hurried out of the shop and across the street to Blackman's.

The bell above the door tinkled as she entered the shop, and the middle-aged man behind the counter looked up. Jane was relieved to see that there were no other customers in the store. The clerk's gaze swept over her assessingly, and Jane knew he was wondering at the appearance of an unescorted young lady in his domain.

"Mr. Johnson at your service. How may I help you?" A true professional, there was nothing in his face or voice to indicate his opinion of his unusual customer.

Jane hesitated for a moment, then walked over to the counter. She withdrew a small, flat box from the pocket of her cloak and placed it on the counter. "I need your help with a delicate matter," she explained. She opened the box with hands that trembled only slightly.

Mr. Johnson's gaze sharpened at the sight of the pearl choker and matching earbobs. A wave of panic swept over Jane, urging her to snatch up the box and leave before it was too late. But she ruthlessly suppressed her feelings, and forced herself to look up at the clerk.

"May I?" he asked.

She nodded, touched by his politeness. Mr. Johnson

lifted the pearl necklace from the case reverently, holding it up to the light, and then examined it from every angle. The earbobs received a similar scrutiny.

With a show of reluctance he returned the jewels to the case. "A most unusual set," he commented. "It isn't often that we see such heirloom pieces." It was not quite a question.

Jane extracted a slip of paper from her reticule. "The proof of ownership is here," she said drily.

"Of course," Mr. Johnson said, but he accepted the certificate nonetheless. Jane gave thanks that she had thought to ask her solicitor Timerson for the certificate, just in case she needed to dispose of the jewels. Without it, none of the reputable shops would deal with her. And the less reputable establishments would take advantage of her by paying less than the jewels were worth.

"Are you looking to sell the jewels outright, or to have us act as your agent?" the clerk enquired. At Jane's blank look he continued, "If we act as your agent, you may obtain a higher sum, but there is no telling how long it will take to find a buyer. Or you can accept a lesser sum, and we will pay you today."

"I have no time to waste," Jane said.

Mr. Johnson nodded, as if unsurprised. Reaching below the counter, he withdrew a piece of paper and a quill pen. Dipping the pen into the inkwell, he wrote a sum on the paper, and then pushed it across the counter. "I think you'll find this a very handsome offer," he said.

Jane examined the sum. One hundred and fifty pounds. It was more than she had hoped for. She was tempted to agree, but common sense told her that no merchant would ever start negotiations by offering his top price.

"Your pen, please," Jane said. Mr. Johnson looked at her quizzically as she scratched out the sum, and wrote the number three hundred below it. "As you said, it is rare to see a set of such quality. I think this is a much more reasonable price."

The clerk looked at her with grudging respect. He stretched his hand out towards the pen she had discarded, and then decided to abandon convention and negotiate directly. "Two hundred pounds," he said, "I really can't offer any more."

"Two hundred guineas," Jane insisted.

"Guineas it is," he agreed. He carefully wrote out a bank draft for the specified amount, and then rang a bell. A young man appeared from the back room, and was given the jewel case containing the pearls, along with instructions to place them in the safe.

"A pleasure doing business with you, miss," Mr. Johnson said, as he handed her the bank draft.

Jane left the shop, torn between joy at having made a good bargain, and the awful feeling that she had betrayed her family by selling their heritage. Even though she knew her mother would support her decision, it still hurt. But there were more important things than jewels. Two hundred guineas was a goodly sum. It was enough to make this quarter's payment on the mortgage. They might even be able to purchase more ewes to replace the ones that had died, although another ram like Percival was out of the question.

The sale of the pearls would not solve their problems, but it bought her a few weeks of time. Time enough to find a more permanent solution. Now all she had to do was find a wealthy husband, and then they need never fear the shadow of poverty again.

For some reason, this thought failed to cheer Jane. It took all her strength to appear unruffled when she collected the boys from the circulating library. Her unsettled mood lasted through the carriage ride home, but the boys took no notice, absorbed in the wondrous sights and sounds of the capital.

The afternoon post brought letters from home, and confirmation that she had made the right decision. Her mother had written to Jane, warning that the boys had taken it in their head to run away, and were probably headed towards London. The letter had apparently been written in great agitation. In one sentence Lady Alice told Jane not to worry herself, that the boys would turn back before they reached York. In a later paragraph she urged Jane to keep her eyes open, and to send word at once when the boys arrived.

Jane's heart went out to her mother, who must be frantic with worry by now. Yesterday, after the twins' unexpected appearance, Jane had sent an express to her mother, to let her know they had arrived safely. But it would be tomorrow at least before the letter arrived. In the meantime her mother could only wait and hope.

The second letter was from her steward, Angus MacLeod. It was blunt and to the point, like the man himself. Matters looked grave, he informed her. In addition to Percival George, the sickness had killed over half their flock. The worst was over now, but it would be a small crop of wool that they would bring to market.

The Bennetts, their former tenants, had left suddenly, one step ahead of the duns. It didn't take long for the news to spread that they had left massive debts behind them. Timerson, their solicitor, had informed them that the Bennetts had not paid the last quarter's rent. In addition to the matter of the rent, they owed the servants back wages.

There's some hard decisions to be made, Miss Jane, Angus wrote, and she could almost hear him speaking the words. If the money couldn't be found to pay the interest on the mortgage, then they would have to sell the Manor and the land. Timerson held out little hope of finding a new tenant in time to do the trick. They could sell their remaining sheep, the sickness ensuring that the local farmers would pay good money to replace their own losses. But if they did that, they sacrificed all hope of future income.

Angus ended the letter with a request for instructions. He could hold things together for another few weeks, but that was all. He closed with best wishes for her health, and success in her London enterprise.

Her "London enterprise" Jane repeated with grim humor. She took it that Angus referred to her attempt to catch a rich husband. Well, no need to tell Angus that she had allowed herself to be distracted by a handsome gentleman who set her pulses racing.

Withdrawing a sheet of parchment from the writing desk, Jane took up her pen and began to write. She started with a letter to Timerson, instructing the solicitor to use the bank draft to pay the mortgage, and to make the balance available for Angus MacLeod. In case her matrimonial plans did not succeed, Jane asked Timerson to find a new tenant.

The letter to Angus was harder to write, because he knew her better, and might read more into the letter than she wanted to reveal. Jane began by informing Angus that she had sold the pearls and sent the draft to Timerson. Angus was to draw on the money to pay the servants their back wages. After all, it was her responsibility that their tenants had proven to be such bounders.

Under no condition, she wrote, was Angus to sell any of the flock. Instead he was to use the balance of the draft as he saw fit. She trusted that he would see things right, until she could make other arrangements. She thought about being more explicit, and then decided that Angus was no fool. He would know what she meant by other arrangements.

The final letter was to her mother. Jane explained the arrangements she had made with Angus and Timerson. She begged her mother's forgiveness for the sale of the pearls, but knew her mother would understand. Lady Alice was not to worry herself, or to let the children fret. Matters were well in hand, and Angus would put things to rights.

Unaccustomed to so much writing, her hand ached when the final letter was finished. Jane rang the bell, then massaged her hand absently. When a footman appeared, Jane handed him the letter for Timerson. "Please see to it that this letter is posted at once. And tell Browning that we will have our tea served here."

"Yes, Miss Sedgwick."

"Does that mean you're finished?" Dick asked. Jane looked across the library to where he and Bobby were lying on the floor in front of the fireplace. They had found a chessboard somewhere, and were engaged in their third game of the afternoon.

"Yes, I am done for now," Jane said, crossing the room to study the game. "Who is winning?"

"I am," Dick replied triumphantly.

"But I won the first game," Bobby countered, jutting out his chin.

"And I won the second," Dick retorted.

"Well, do you think you could tear yourselves away from the game long enough to have some tea?"

The boys jumped up with an enthusiasm that sent the pieces flying. "Gently, gently," she admonished them. "Pick up the game first and return it to where you found it."

The task was accomplished just as the tea cart was wheeled in. Jane served the boys, and then gave them the final bit of news. "The arrangements have been made. You will be going home tomorrow on the mail coach."

"Tomorrow?" Bobby complained. "But we just got here."

"Yes," Jane said. "And you should never have come. I had a letter from Mama. She is beside herself with worry."

"But you sent her a letter, so she'll know we're fine," Dick countered.

"Still, this is no place for you. Lady Barton has been very gracious—"

"Humph!" Bobby said, making a face to indicate his opinion of Lady Barton's graciousness.

"As I said, Lady Barton has been gracious enough to let you stay here. But you can't stay here forever, and you are needed back home."

Dick nodded, accepting this bit of logic.

"Lord Glendale has made all the arrangements. He's sending Mr. Stapleton, his secretary, along to see that you get home safely." And to see that you go straight home without further delay, Jane added to herself.

Glendale's note had mentioned that Stapleton had business in York, so it was no trouble for him to accompany the boys. This was patently absurd, but it was typical of Glendale to downplay his generosity. Her heart filled with warmth at the thought of his kindness. He was a good friend.

In her heart she knew that he could have been more than just a friend. If only she had more time, time for her to be sure of her feelings, and to find out if he returned her affection. But there was no time. She might as well wish that her father was still alive, or that they had never heard of the feckless Mr. Cartwright.

"Everything will be all right now, won't it Jane?" Dick asked anxiously.

Jane looked at her brother curiously. This was the first time one of them had referred to the reasons for their mad jaunt, since their arrival. The boys had been in such high spirits, it seemed as if they had forgotten all about the trouble at home. She supposed it was a compliment that they placed so much trust in her ability to make matters right.

"Everything will be fine. As long as you don't take it in your heads to leave home again."

The boys nodded vigorously. "We promise to be good. We'll never get in trouble again."

Jane bit back a smile. The twins were sincere, but never was a very long time. Still they were good lads, and deserved a better life than their family had been able to provide. With a little resolution, she could provide for them, and for all her brothers and sisters. It was time that she stopped thinking of her own happiness, and started thinking of her family instead.

Chapter Nine

Glendale puzzled over the mystery of Miss Sedgwick. She had been acting oddly ever since the arrival of her brothers. And just what was the message they had conveyed to her? Who was this Percival George, and why should it matter that he was dead? Why would her brothers rush to bring her the news, against the wishes of their mother?

A relative? No, she had denied it, and the boys, while concerned, had not seemed grief-stricken. But Jane had been shocked by the news, however much she tried to hide it. Could this Percival be a suitor? Some country clodhopper to whom she had formed an ineligible attachment? Had her family sent her to London, in the hopes of preventing an improper romance?

He knew that he was grasping at straws, but he couldn't put the puzzle out of his mind. Percival George. The name conjured up images of a weedy young cleric, peering shortsightedly over his spectacles. The picture of Jane with such a man was laughable.

But in his mind the picture changed, and he saw Jane

in the embrace of a well-favored, virile young Squire. It was hard to think that Jane might prefer her rustic swain to the cultured gentlemen she met in London. But Jane had never been predictable. She appeared to set no store by the conventions that the *ton* prized. No doubt this Percival had shared her enthusiasms for agriculture and the land. Glendale scowled, prompting those standing near him to take a step back.

Only Freddie was brave enough to approach. "Up to your old tricks, sulking in the corners, I see. Can't you come to a function and act civil for once?"

"I was not sulking," Glendale said. "I was merely considering my stupidity in coming here in the first place." His gaze swept restlessly over the packed drawing room. The cream of society was packed into Mrs. Elliot's town house tonight, making her rout the shocking squeeze that all good hostesses longed for. In the close quarters the heat was proving unbearable, and Glendale tugged irritably at his collar, wondering how much longer he would have to wait for his quarry to appear.

"In that case, why don't you leave? There are a dozen other hostesses who would be delighted if you graced them with your presence."

"Why don't *you* leave?" Glendale countered.

"Can't." Lord Frederick nodded his head to where his sister stood chatting with her friends. "Promised my mother I'd do the pretty tonight, and take Priscilla around." He took a sip of champagne before adding, "I never thought I'd be done in by a sixteen-year-old girl. Where the chit gets her energy, I don't know. This is the third function we've been to tonight."

Glendale nodded absently, his attention on the guests who had just arrived. Even across the room, her unusual height made it possible to spot Jane, as she and Lady Barton stopped to greet their hostess. Strange, he never noticed how tall she was when he was with her. It was only when he saw her from a distance that he was struck by her height.

"Here, make yourself useful for once," Glendale said, handing his half-full glass to Freddie. Without waiting for a response he made his way over to the door. Long experience with these affairs made him adept at weaving through the crowds. Nodding in response to greetings, he resisted all attempts by distant acquaintances to trap him into a conversation. With a feeling of satisfaction he arrived at the entrance just as Jane and Lady Barton finished paying their respects.

"Good evening, Lady Barton, Miss Sedgwick," he said. "What a pleasant surprise to encounter you here." Surprise indeed. He had been cooling his heels here for the last hour, knowing that Lady Barton's long friendship with Mrs. Elliot meant that she would surely make an appearance tonight.

Jane murmured some suitable response, but her smile seemed forced. Looking closely he could see the lines of strain around her eyes.

Lady Barton was still talking with Mrs. Elliot, so Glendale seized the initiative. "Miss Sedgwick, Miss Blake was just mentioning how much she hoped to see you this evening. With your permission, I will escort you over to her."

With a quick bow, Glendale tucked Jane's hand into his arm, and led her away.

"But I don't want to see Miss Blake," Jane protested.

"Of course you don't. But I couldn't think of any other excuse. And given half a chance, Lady Barton would have stood there prosing for hours."

"Oh," Jane said with a weak smile. "Then I thank you for intervention. It was lucky for me that you happened by."

Luck had nothing to do with it, but he wasn't about to confess that he had been waiting here hoping to see her. It might give her the wrong idea.

Glendale led Jane through the crowd, intent on putting as much space between them and Lady Barton as possible. He found a secluded spot, near the open French windows that led out to the terrace. The cool night breezes from the terrace provided a welcome relief from the overheated ballroom.

Snagging two gilt chairs from against the wall, he held one for Jane to sit in, and then sat down beside her. Jane glanced around, apparently surprised by their relative isolation. New to London as she was, she didn't realize that it was always possible to be private, even in the most crowded of functions.

Glendale examined her with a critical eye, wondering at her subdued manner. The lavender silk gown that she wore showed off her youthful figure to perfection, although the fashionable neckline showed far too much creamy bosom. A silver pendant drew attention to her *décolletage.*

Even the highest stickler could find no fault with her appearance, but the spark, the animation that made her memorable, was lacking. She had lost that which transformed her from an ordinary young woman into an Incomparable.

He noticed again the sadness in her eyes, and determined to get to the bottom of this puzzle. "I hope you don't mind, but I wanted to have a chance to talk with you, before your admirers claimed you," Glendale began, gesturing with his hand to indicate the crowded room. His strategic retreat had bought them a little time, but before long the bolder among her admirers would seek them out. After all, the purpose of a rout was to see and be seen, as you exchanged the latest gossip with your acquaintances. And the opportunity to be seen with a reigning beauty was not to be missed.

"No, I am glad that we have this opportunity," Jane said. "I want to thank you for your kindness to me and

my brothers. I don't know how I would have managed without your help."

Glendale accepted her thanks, although his conscience whispered that she wouldn't be nearly as grateful if she knew of Stapleton's private instructions.

An awkward silence fell between them. Jane opened her mouth as if to speak, and then closed it, prompting him to ask, "Is everything all right?"

"Why wouldn't it be?" Jane replied sharply.

Glendale looked at her steadily, but she blushed, and lowered her head, refusing to meet his gaze. "Because you look as if something is troubling you," he continued.

Jane took a deep breath and unclenched her fists. With one hand she smoothed down her skirt.

"Lady Barton has warned me about spending too much time with you," Jane said, *a propos* of nothing.

"Why on earth would she do that?"

Jane finally turned the force of her gaze on him. An undefinable emotion clouded her normally clear green eyes. "Because you aren't the kind of man that I need."

"And what kind of man is that?" he asked, trying to make sense of this bizarre conversation.

"The kind that will marry me," Jane stated baldly. His features must have registered his disbelief, because she continued in a patient tone. "Everyone says that you aren't in the market for a wife. And my time in London is too short to waste."

Glendale felt a slow rage building inside him. To think that he had waited here for hours, just to catch a glimpse of her. That he had spent the last days wondering how he could help her. How dare she insult him. "Waste? Is that how you think of the time we spent together? How could I have been so mistaken as to think that you enjoyed my company?"

Miss Sedgwick appeared oblivious to his sarcasm. "Yes, but don't you see? That is the trouble. I let myself get caught up in the excitement, and forgot the reason why I was here."

The impudence of the chit passed all belief. Here she was, laying bare the whole of her coldhearted scheme with a logic that would have done credit to the most mercenary of females. It was difficult to believe that he had been so mistaken in her character.

"Forgive me," he said stiffly. "I didn't mean to interfere with your schemes."

"Of course if you were interested in me, it would be different," Miss Sedgwick said softly.

"I am afraid you'll have to seek another pigeon for your little game," Glendale said cuttingly, trying to control the urge to wrap his hands around her deceitful little neck. Rising swiftly he made her a mocking bow. "I will leave you to your hunting, Miss Sedgwick."

With that he strode away, abandoning Miss Sedgwick to her own devices. It was bad manners, but nothing compared to what he really wanted to do to her. Once again he had been deceived by a female, and he could feel the rage pounding in his chest.

He headed for the door, intent on putting as much space between himself and that callous vixen as he could. But before he reached the door, he spotted Lord Frederick talking with several of his friends. Glendale changed direction and headed over to them.

"I'll expect your cheque in the morning," Glendale said bluntly.

"Cheque?"

"The hundred pounds," Glendale elaborated. "It has been four weeks now, and Miss Sedgwick is the epitome of a society lady. Avaricious, grasping, deceitful, and intent only on trapping some helpless fellow into matrimony. A remarkable transformation indeed."

Freddie glanced over at Lord David Cartland and Mr.

Helprin, who were taking this in with interest. "Glendale, you can't mean what you are saying."

"On the contrary," Glendale replied, heedless of the eager audience. "You can count yourself lucky that she didn't set her cap at you instead." With that he turned on his heel and left the Elliots' town house.

Walking outside to his carriage, Glendale reflected bitterly on the unfaithfulness of the female sex. To think that he had once again been taken in by a pretty face and engaging manner. You would think he would have learned his lesson years ago, after that fiasco with Miss Julia Hanscombe. But no. Like a callow youth he had allowed himself to be blinded by Miss Sedgwick's seemingly artless charm and winning ways.

He had to give her credit though. An actress of her caliber should be treading the boards of Drury Lane. Mentally he reviewed the events of the past month, seeing everything now through a different light. How she must have laughed at him as she played the part of the naive country lass.

Her only miscalculation was in revealing her hand too soon. She must have decided to break the connection, once she realized that she had no hope of engaging his affections. It was fortunate for him that she had done so before his heart was involved.

Never again. From now on he would confine his attentions to those women who were honest about bartering their favors. Rapping on the coach roof, he directed the coachman to Violetta Archer's residence. He had been neglecting her for these last weeks, but it was time now to make amends. At least there he could be sure of his welcome.

But when he arrived, he found the welcome was not what he had envisioned. It took several minutes for a maid to answer his knock.

"Oh, milord, we didn't expect you," the maid said anxiously. She held the door, as if undecided whether or not to let him in. Glendale brushed by her and entered the hall. The maid darted past him to the foot of the stairs. "I'll just tell Mrs. Archer that you're here," she said.

Something was amiss. At this hour of the evening, Violetta was normally to be found downstairs in her salon. Even if she was upstairs, it was out of character for her not to rush to greet him. Glendale's gaze swept the hall, pausing briefly as he noted the presence of a gentleman's hat and gloves on the hall table. An ebony walking stick was propped next to them.

The maid blanched as she followed his gaze. "I'll tell Mrs. Archer you've come, milord," she repeated desperately.

"No need," Glendale said. "I appear to have made a mistake."

He let himself out, and returned to his carriage. "I've changed my mind, Barnes," he said to the curious coachman. "Take me home."

"Yes, my lord," Barnes said, without a trace of expression.

In the library of his town house, Glendale poured himself a snifter of brandy, then settled himself in a chair by the fire. A single candle branch provided the only illumination, but the darkness suited his mood.

Placing the glass on the table, he reached up and untied his cravat. Then he took a sip of brandy, cradling the glass in his hands as he thought of the wrongs that had been done to him.

Jane and Violetta. Before this evening he would have sworn that they were as different as two women could be, yet they had both betrayed him. Violetta had cause at least. After his shocking neglect, it was no wonder that she had sought another protector. Violetta had probably assumed that it was only a matter of time before he cast her over.

And Jane. He would have taken an oath that she didn't

have a deceitful bone in her body. His heart felt heavy, and he told himself it was anger at her treachery. But it didn't feel like anger. It felt like sadness. He had liked the girl. Glendale laughed mirthlessly as he realized that earlier this evening he had been worried about her. Worried that something might be wrong, and wondering how he could help.

But she hadn't needed his help. Hadn't wanted it. He was just a tool to be used, then discarded, in her matrimonial quest. No doubt a mere Viscount was too lowly for her ambitions. Well, he wished her luck. Let her make some other poor sod miserable. He was happy to be well out of her clutches.

Jane checked the impulse to run after Matthew. She knew she had made a botch of her explanation. When faced with his presence, her carefully rehearsed speeches had been forgotten. Instead her desperation had gotten the better of her, and she blurted out the first thing that came to mind. Had she really told him she had no time to waste with him? She cringed at the memory of the anger on his face. What must he be thinking of her now? Belatedly Jane realized that she had taken her anger at her circumstances out on Matthew.

She could try to explain, but to what purpose? He would never understand unless she laid bare the whole of her plight. And she had too much pride to do that. She wanted more from Glendale than his friendship, or worse yet, his pity. But Matthew had made it clear that he had no intention of offering more.

So be it then. Without the distraction of his attentions, she could turn her thoughts to her purpose. Rising from the chair, Jane searched the room, looking for a likely prospect. Spotting Mr. Joyce in conversation with Miss

Grimes, whom she knew slightly, Jane made her way over towards them.

"Miss Sedgwick, how thrilling to see you," Miss Grimes said. From the enthusiasm of her greeting, Jane could only conclude that Mr. Joyce had been boring Miss Grimes to tears. "And of course, you know Mr. Joyce."

"Your servant, Miss Sedgwick," said Mr. Joyce, turning his torso to face her, the high points of his collar making it impossible for him to turn his head.

"Are you here on your own?" Miss Grimes enquired.

"No, Lady Barton accompanied me," Jane replied, wondering at the odd question.

Miss Grimes plied her ivory fan languidly. In her third season she was the epitome of elegant sophistication, and Jane began to feel uncertain of herself in a way that she had not felt since the night of her ball.

"Of course. I just wondered, since Lord Glendale left so suddenly." Miss Grimes gave Jane a look of such pure sympathy that it had to be contrived.

Jane didn't bother replying to the barb. Something was going on. Normally she had to simply make an appearance at a ball or rout to find herself surrounded by admirers. It was the reason why Glendale had led her away to a secluded spot for their tête à tête. Jane had hated the attention, yet now that it was gone, she missed it. She suddenly felt alone and vulnerable.

"Excuse me, ladies," Mr. Joyce said abruptly, and with a jerky bow he was gone.

Miss Grimes chattered on about her successes, and Jane listened with half an ear as she tried to figure out what was different this evening. The space around her and Miss Grimes widened imperceptibly, until they stood isolated among the chattering throng. Looking at the faces around them, Jane imagined that they were looking at her, talking about her.

Nonsense. Her nerves were merely overset after the

scene with Glendale. Jane pressed one hand to her throbbing temples. The heat and noisy crowd was suddenly too much to bear.

"Pray excuse me, Miss Grimes. I see my aunt signalling for me," Jane lied.

Miss Grimes arched her eyebrows in polite disbelief. "Of course," she replied, turning her gaze significantly to where Lady Barton stood chattering with several older ladies. Lady Barton's back was to them, so there was no way she could have been signalling.

Jane made a hasty retreat. Her head was beginning to pound in earnest. She went over to where Lady Barton was standing, hoping to convince her aunt to leave early.

The ladies tittered, and Jane found time to wonder what it was that they found so amusing. She arrived in time to hear Mrs. Dunne say, "And I heard Lord Cartland say that it was all a silly wager. Glendale had no more interest in her than a flea."

Jane stopped a few paces away, rooted to the spot. A wager?

"And was it true that he called her a fortune hunter?" another lady asked.

"I heard that he called her a grasping harpy," replied another.

"It must all be a mistake," Mrs. Elliot said. "After all, Letitia, she is your niece. I can't imagine that she would forget herself so."

Her niece. Jane realized that they were talking about her. What had Glendale said?

The ladies looked at Lady Barton, and Jane waited for her aunt to defend her.

"Well, I always knew that girl would be trouble," Lady Barton said with a heavy sigh. "But Lord Barton insisted that I do my duty and sponsor her. Why he even put up the dowry so she could make a respectable match. I told Barton that she would come to no good, but he wouldn't listen." Lady Barton paused while her friends made commiserating noises. "Cornelia's as unruly as her mother. I offered to find my niece a decent match, but she had her eyes set higher. Well, she looks a pretty fool now that Glendale's discovered her ruse."

Jane's spirits plummeted, and she longed for the floor to open up and swallow her. But there was no such luck. One of the ladies surrounding her aunt spotted Jane, and nudged her companion with her fan, pointing in Jane's direction.

In that moment she hated them all. She hated her aunt, London, and the whole of society. She even hated Matthew for his careless comments that had destroyed her peace.

Her hatred gave her the strength to raise her chin and approach her aunt. "Lady Barton," Jane said, touching her aunt's sleeve to get her attention.

Lady Barton whirled, startled by Jane's sudden appearance. A dull mottled flush spread over her face as Lady Barton realized that Jane had heard her last remarks.

"I have the headache, and would like to retire," Jane said firmly. "That is, if you are agreeable, dear aunt?"

Lady Barton glanced at Jane, and evidently decided not to risk a public confrontation. "Of course," Lady Barton said.

Jane swept out of the room, glancing back only once to ensure that Lady Barton was following her. They waited in arctic silence as the footman helped them into their capes, and then waited for their carriage to arrive.

Once they were in the privacy of the carriage, Lady Barton made one attempt to break the silence.

"Your behavior this evening was most exceptionable," Lady Barton said. "Going off into a corner for a coze with Lord Glendale, and then dragging me out of there without a by-your-leave. I don't wonder what people will say."

How dare her aunt attempt to lecture her? The hypocrisy sickened Jane. "On the contrary, I know exactly what they will say. After all, I heard you and your friends dissecting my character quite thoroughly."

"You impertinent—"

"Enough." Jane said, weary of the whole evening. "If you and the faithless Glendale are any example of town manners, then I am grateful to have been raised in the country."

"How dare you take that tone with me?" Lady Barton blustered.

"I will speak to you any way I please," Jane shot back. "I have had enough of your hypocritical lectures. If you wish me to be polite, then I suggest you remain silent."

Of course Lady Barton ignored Jane's wishes, and continued to lecture her niece on her lack of breeding for the rest of the drive home. Jane paid no attention, letting her aunt's words wash over her like an angry sea.

She had room in her mind for only one thought. Matthew had betrayed her. He had interpreted her words as a slight, and then taken a swift revenge. It didn't matter what he had actually said. Whether he had called her a fortune hunter, or a harpy, or an ill-mannered chit, the effect was all the same. She was ruined. He had given the *ton* a juicy scandal, and in a few days there wouldn't be a soul in society who hadn't heard the news.

Jane had seen how quickly society could turn on a favorite. Her fickle admirers would disappear like the mist. In a single evening she had gone from being Miss Sedgwick the Incomparable, to Miss Sedgwick the fortune hunter. In one stroke Glendale had destroyed her chance to make an eligible alliance, and her family's last hope for security. She hoped his revenge brought him no satisfaction.

Chapter Ten

"Lady Barton and Miss Sedgwick," intoned the liveried footman as he ushered them into Mrs. Hatcher's salon. The room fell silent as everyone turned to stare at the newcomers.

"Is she the one?" screeched the elderly Lady Archer, who was widely known in society for both her deafness and her lack of tact. Jane pretended not to have heard, plastering a tranquil expression on her face as she greeted Mrs. Hatcher, and then took a seat as far away from Lady Archer as possible.

But Lady Archer was hard to ignore. "You say Glendale paid her a hundred pounds? Whatever for?" Lady Archer demanded. Mrs. Willoughby, Lady Archer's much-tried daughter, tried to silence her mother, but to no avail.

Jane's seat placed her near the Simpson sisters who giggled nervously, and then began babbling about their recent shopping expedition. They made no attempt to include Jane in the conversation, for which she was grateful. Was it possible for one's face to freeze into a permanent insincere smile? Jane suspected that she was likely to find out.

It was her own fault, of course. Lady Barton had taken gleeful pleasure in warning her that it would be like this. But Jane had insisted on accompanying her aunt as Lady Barton made her round of calls. Jane had been unwilling to give up without a fight. She had cherished the hope that matters were not as grim as they had first appeared on that awful night. But that hope was quickly dashed. Wherever Jane went, she found herself the recipient of sly glances and the subject of whispered conversations. Some ladies didn't even bother to whisper, as witness the unfortunate Lady Archer.

Jane glanced at the ormolu clock on the mantelpiece. To her horror only five minutes had passed since they entered. It would be at least another twenty before they could take their leave. And it was no use counting on Lady Barton to rescue her. On the contrary, her aunt was enjoying her role in this drama.

Jane now realized how much her aunt had resented Jane's earlier successes. After all, hadn't she heard Lady Barton telling her friends that she had never wanted to sponsor Jane in the first place? Her invitation to Jane had been prompted by Lord Barton's threat to invite the entire family to come live with them. No wonder Lady Barton had been furious when Jane refused her first offer.

But now everything was turning out as Lady Barton had hoped. Jane had been rejected by polite society, and no one could lay the fault at her aunt's door. In a strange way, Lady Barton had finally achieved her revenge on her beautiful sister Alice.

But even Lady Barton didn't realize how complete her victory was. When he made her an outcast, Lord Glendale had done more than destroy Jane's happiness. He had robbed her of the chance to save her family from the ruin that now threatened. Bitterness filled her heart at the thought of the treacherous Lord Glendale. How could she have put her trust in such a man?

It was mortifying to realize how thoroughly he had duped her. She had believed his honeyed lies. She had thought him a friend, someone who cared for her. She had lived with the hope that one day he might see her as something more than a friend.

Even after her humiliation at the ball, Jane had still believed in him. After the first shock wore off, she convinced herself that it was all a misunderstanding. Surely Glendale couldn't have said those callous words. Jane had waited anxiously for Glendale to call.

But Glendale hadn't called. Actually no one had called, but it was Glendale's absence that had destroyed her faith. Never before had he failed to call on her after seeing her at a gathering. His failure to do so was confirmation of his guilt. To think, all the time she had called him friend, he had been playing with her. Laughing at her. Leading her on until he tired of the game, and destroyed her reputation with a few well-chosen phrases.

Jane could think of no reason for his actions. She had done Lord Glendale no wrong. Perhaps it was not malice that prompted his actions, but boredom. His attentions might have been caused by the overpowering ennui that was said to be the bane of the nobility's existence. Glendale may have seen her as a diversion. She had amused him for a time, and when she ceased to be amusing, he dismissed her.

Neither explanation satisfied her, but it didn't really matter. Now she had to deal with the consequences of Glendale's actions. It was the ultimate unfairness that his reputation should remain spotless. Glendale was the deceiver and betrayer, yet no stain fell upon his honor. Only Jane, his innocent dupe, would suffer.

Jane endured the rest of their half hour at Mrs. Hatcher's with grim determination. She refused to let these society tabbies think that they had cowed her. During the carriage ride home Lady Barton made several attempts at conversation, but Jane refused to be drawn. As soon as they reached the town house, Jane escaped to the privacy of her own room.

The problem of her future was now pressing. And Jane had seen for herself that there was little chance that society would let her back in its good graces. At least not for some time to come. And time was the one thing she didn't have.

It was less than a week since she had sent the twins back to Yorkshire, but it seemed like a lifetime to Jane. A week ago she had been confident that she could solve their problems by making an advantageous marriage. Several of her suitors had hinted that they were willing to make an offer. All she'd needed to do was make her choice.

But she had been unwilling to choose, and this, too, was Glendale's fault. Jane laughed bitterly as she remembered her foolish hopes. Strange now to think that she had once considered him the most wonderful of men. She had preferred his company above all others, feeling complete only when she was with him. She had deluded herself into thinking the attraction mutual, and spurned her other suitors in favor of spending more time with Glendale.

Well, she was paying for her vanity now. Not one of her erstwhile suitors had called in the days since Mrs. Elliot's ball. She had gone from having too many choices to having none at all. It was a dilemma with no solution, but Jane refused to give up. "There must be a way," she vowed. "I will find a way out of this fix, and be damned to Lord Glendale."

Glendale skimmed the morning paper with idle curiosity, but nothing caught his interest, and he tossed it aside irritably. Reaching down for his china cup, he took a sip of coffee. The coffee was lukewarm and bitter. He glanced at the silver coffeepot, but no doubt the liquid it contained was no better.

"Fisk!" Glendale shouted, ignoring the brass bell that was supposed to be used to summon the servants.

A young man in livery entered the room. "Yes, milord?" he asked anxiously. Fisk's manner annoyed Glendale. There was no reason for the man to look like a frightened rabbit.

Glendale pointed to the offending object. "Take this swill away and fetch me some real coffee. And be quick about it."

"Yes, milord. At once, milord," Fisk replied, removing the silver pot. He returned scant moments later, bearing a new pot. Selecting a fresh cup and saucer from the sideboard, Fisk carefully poured out a new cup of coffee, then waited for Glendale's nod of approval.

"Will there be anything else, milord?" Fisk asked.

"No," Glendale said shortly, waving the man off. Why on earth did Fisk insist on hovering so?

Glendale reached for the paper, before remembering that he had already discarded it. He glanced at the wall clock. It was just on nine o'clock. For the first time in weeks he had the leisure to enjoy his breakfast in peace. Now that the wager had been won, his life was once more his own. No more wasting his time squiring a young lady around London. No more trips to the galleries and museums and the fashionable spots of London. No more morning calls on tiresome biddies, or evenings spent in the company of the most respectable and boring members of London society.

He had waited weeks for this day. He should be rejoicing. But instead all that he felt was a nameless irritation. He should be happy to be free from Miss Sedgwick's clutches. Glendale cast his mind back to Saturday's ball, trying to recapture his earlier feelings of righteous indignation. But as he imagined Jane's face, all he could feel was a sense of loss.

Glendale set his cup down with a suddenness that made the china rattle. He couldn't be missing the chit. She was a coldhearted schemer. Her own words had condemned her. It was true that he had enjoyed her company, but she was nothing special. Glendale squirmed mentally, unwilling to examine that thought too closely.

He was saved from further introspection by the arrival of his butler with the morning post. Glendale flipped through the invitations, not bothering to open them. Tucked among the missives was an envelope that bore Freddie's distinctive scrawl.

A piece of paper fluttered out as Glendale tore open the envelope. Picking up the paper, he found it was a bank draft for the sum of one hundred pounds. What the devil? Frederick's note was equally cryptic. *In payment of my debt of honor. Your servant, Lord Frederick, et cetera.*

Now what maggot had gotten into Freddie's skull? Why would he mail the draft, rather than delivering it himself? And what did he mean by the tone of that letter? Glendale had received tradesman's bills that contained more warmth. Only Freddie could give him the answers he sought, and Glendale decided to seek his friend out.

It took most of the day for Glendale to track his friend down. Glendale had called at Freddie's rooms, only to be told that Lord Frederick had just left. Freddie's valet vouchsafed the information that his master had mentioned calling on his tailor, but it was all a hum, as when Glendale called on Weston, he found that Freddie was not there, nor was he expected to be.

Glendale finally ran his friend to ground at White's. Entering the main room, Glendale spied Mr. Charles Givens in his usual spot by the fire. Charles Givens was a permanent fixture at the club, there at all hours of the day and night. A popular rumur had it that Givens hadn't set foot outside of the club in twenty years. Glendale knew that for a lie, having once encountered Givens in the City. But it was still a good story, and when Givens was at White's, he served as the unofficial doorkeeper.

"Good afternoon, Charlie," Glendale greeted him. "Have you seen Freddie today?"

"Afternoon, Glendale," Givens growled from behind his paper, without bothering to look up. "You'll find Lord Frederick in the card room with Mountjoy."

Glendale thanked him for the information and headed for the card room. He spotted Freddie easily, the card room being mostly empty at this hour of the afternoon. Freddie was in conversation with Mountjoy, as they watched a desultory round of whist.

"Afternoon, Freddie," Glendale said. "I've spent half the day looking for you, and worn out my best boots. Where have you been hiding yourself?"

Freddie appeared startled to see him. "I regret having caused you such inconvenience, Lord Glendale," he said stiffly.

Glendale stared at his friend. What was wrong with him? "Mountjoy, I'm certain you will excuse us," Glendale said, grabbing Freddie by one arm. Without waiting for a response, he dragged his friend over to a secluded spot by the window.

"What has gotten into you, Freddie? And since when did you start calling me Lord Glendale?"

Freddie minced no words. "No *Friend* of mine would have behaved so badly."

Glendale shook his head, hoping that would clear the confusion. "What are you talking about?"

"Miss Sedgwick," Freddie said.

"What about her?"

Freddie gestured impatiently. "Miss Sedgwick? Mrs. Elliot's ball? Where you publicly branded the poor girl a heartless schemer?" Freddie finished by crossing his arms and looked at him challengingly.

"And if I did? It's the truth, isn't it?" Glendale said.

"So you say now. But a few days ago you were singing her praises."

He couldn't believe that Freddie was taking Miss Sedgwick's side. Had she worked her wiles on him as well? "I was wrong," Glendale said tightly. "She admitted it herself, saying that she needed to marry a wealthy lord, and had no time for someone like myself." Glendale's conscience pricked him a little at the exaggeration. Miss Sedgwick hadn't exactly said those words, but he knew that's what she had meant.

"So that's it. She pricked your pride, and you retaliated."

Freddie's words stung. They couldn't possibly be true. Glendale's anger had been caused by his failure to see through her deception earlier. "What does it matter what I said?"

"We should never have made that damnable wager," Freddie said, turning his head to look out the window in apparent fascination. "No gentleman makes a wager involving a lady." Freddie turned back to look at Glendale, and the anger in his face was clear to see. "Or at the very least, you could have kept your mouth shut. There was no need to mention it in front of witnesses. The news of the bet was all over London within the day."

Glendale opened his mouth to reply, then shut it. There was no defense he could make. Freddie was right. The wager had been a breach of the unwritten rules that governed the *ton*. By now Miss Sedgwick's reputation was in tatters. She would be lucky if she was received anywhere publicly again. He felt a twinge of unease at that thought, and tried to convince himself that he didn't care what happened to Jane.

"After all, she brought it on herself," Glendale finally replied.

"Yes, as a matter of fact she did," Freddie answered. "She should have known better than to consort with two reprobates like ourselves. Too bad no one thought to warn her." Rising from the chair, he paused for a last word. "For my part, I've grown to like Miss Sedgwick. And, schemer or not, she didn't deserve what we did to her."

Glendale sat for a few minutes after Freddie had left. He tried to convince himself that Freddie would soon get over his anger. Surely Freddie wouldn't throw away years of friendship over a silly quarrel about a woman.

Women. They were the bane of the male sex, Glendale concluded, as he left White's environs. Not a one of them was to be trusted. Look at Miss Sedgwick. Or his former fiancée Miss Hanscombe. Or even Violetta, his erstwhile mistress.

Thoughts of Violetta reminded him that he had yet to inform her that the liaison was over. He could send a note, but that would be too cold. After all, the rupture was partly his fault. He had been too caught up in his supposed courtship of Miss Sedgwick to spare any time for his mistress. Small wonder that Violetta had sought another protector. The least he could do was send her a parting gift with his message.

It was nearly dark, and the clerk was preparing to close the shop when Glendale arrived at Blackman's. But at the sight of a noble client, the clerk hurriedly opened the door.

"Lord Glendale, what a privilege to see you again," Mr. Johnson said, rushing out from the back room. Mr. Johnson waved one hand at the clerk, who immediately began relighting the lamps that had been extinguished earlier.

"I need a gift for a . . . friend," Glendale said.

"Of course, my lord," said Mr. Johnson smoothly. "And is there anything in particular you had in mind?"

Something that she can easily pawn in case of need,

Glendale thought. But he didn't voice the thought aloud, giving in to Mr. Johnson's attempt to preserve appearances. Glendale didn't mind. He valued the staff at Blackman's for their discretion. Unlike the more fashionable Rundell's, no word of this transaction would reach the gossips.

"I have a set of rubies here that are very nice," the clerk said, lifting them out from the display case.

Glendale admired the rubies, but decided against them. Rubies were for passion, and his passion for Violetta had died long ago.

"Perhaps a diamond collar?" Mr. Johnson suggested. Glendale gave a brief glance at the item in question. It was perfect. It was gaudy and tasteless, and Violetta would undoubtedly love it.

"Fine. I'll take it," Glendale said. Borrowing a pen, he scratched out a quick missive, and then sealed the note and wrote Violetta's direction on the front. "Have it sent round to this address."

"Very good, my lord," Mr. Johnson said. "I am certain your friend will be delighted with your choice."

She should be, Glendale thought. The collar had set him back nearly three hundred pounds. Gathering his gloves and hat, he prepared to leave, when an object under the counter caught his eye.

"What's that?" he asked.

Johnson looked down, following his glance. "Oh that. It's a very fine matched set of pearls we just received in."

"May I see them?" Glendale demanded. There was something about those pearls that struck a chord in his memory.

Johnson hesitated, then removed the tray from under the glass case. "These pearls are very fine indeed. Especially if you are considering a gift for a young lady," he said.

From the way the clerk stressed the words young lady, Glendale realized that Johnson was trying to hint that the pearls were not at all the thing to be presented to a member of the *demi-monde.* "No, no, the collar is fine," Glendale reassured the clerk. "I just wanted to see this."

Glendale picked up the pearl necklace and turned it over in his hands. It was a lovely piece, set in the old-fashioned style of his grandmother's day. It was strangely familiar, and he closed his eyes, trying to remember where he had seen them before. The image of Jane came to him, smiling up at him in happiness as they danced at her come-out ball. She had worn pearls much like this around her slender neck, and the earbobs had danced in accompaniment to her laughter.

Glendale dropped the necklace as if it burned.

"Is something wrong, my lord?" Johnson asked.

"No," Glendale said shortly. This business with Miss Sedgwick had addled his brains. It was just a set of pearls. Hundreds of women had similar sets all over the country. There was no reason why they should remind him of her. Miss Sedgwick was nothing to him. In a few weeks he would be hard-pressed to recall her name or her features. And that would suit him just fine.

Chapter Eleven

"Mr. Whitmore to see Miss Sedgwick," intoned the officious Browning.

Jane looked up in surprise. She hadn't expected any callers, not after that dreadful scene two days ago at Mrs. Hatcher's. Even Lady Barton's acquaintances had ceased to visit. Mr. Whitmore was the first visitor in days. Unless you counted Lord Frederick, of course. He had made a brief call to apologize for any distress that he and Lord Glendale may have caused her. Lord Frederick had seemed genuinely contrite, and she forgave him his minor role immediately. But it was an extremely awkward visit. The real culprit, Lord Glendale, was nowhere to be seen. Lord Frederick's apology only served to spotlight Glendale's continued absence.

Jane thrust the treacherous Glendale from her thoughts, and rose to greet her caller.

"Mr. Whitmore," she said. "What a pleasant surprise."

"Your servant, Miss Sedgwick," Mr. Whitmore replied, crossing the room and taking her hand in greeting. Behind him, Browning made a point of leaving the door open, since Jane had no chaperone. Jane had scarcely resumed her own seat when her maid Sally scuttled in. Sally gave a quick curtsey, and then sat on a bench in the back, trying her best to look invisible. Browning appeared intent on preserving whatever shreds were left of Jane's reputation.

"I trust I did not disturb you," Whitmore said, after a moment of silence had passed.

"On the contrary, your company is a welcome relief from my own thoughts." It was the simple truth. Earlier this morning Jane had decided that it was no use staying in London. Her best course was to return home, and to help Angus MacLeod salvage what he could of their fortunes. All that remained now was to inform Lady Barton of her decision, so Jane had been sitting here, impatiently waiting for Lady Barton to return from her shopping.

Mr. Whitmore's gaze swept the room. "I must confess, I did not expect to be so fortunate as to find you alone. The last time I called, you were surrounded by admirers."

"Well, as you can see, that is no longer a problem. It seems I am quite out of fashion." Jane's pride still stung over the defection of her one-time suitors.

"Well, I am neither young nor wellborn, but if an elderly admirer would suit, I gladly offer myself in that role."

"You are not elderly," Jane protested, for lack of anything else to say. It was true, she thought, looking up at his kindly face. Mr. Whitmore's hair was more gray than brown, but he was still a vigorous man. She hadn't thought of him in terms of a suitor, but it wasn't that improbable. True, he was twenty years her senior. But girls younger than she married older titled lords all the time. Twenty years wasn't a large gap, in the eyes of society.

Her answer seemed to please him, for he smiled back at her, and Jane found herself basking in the friendliness of that smile. It seemed ages since she had seen a friendly face.

"There is a special reason why I called on you this morning," Mr. Whitmore continued. "I wonder if I might have a moment of private conversation." With a nod of his head, he indicated the silently watchful maid.

Jane was well and truly puzzled now. But she trusted Mr. Whitmore, so she didn't hesitate. "Sally, I believe you are needed upstairs," Jane said firmly.

"But Mr. Browning said—"

"Enough. Please attend to your tasks upstairs."

Sally got up, a mutinous expression on her normally placid countenance. The maid walked with deliberate slowness to the door, then hesitated on the threshold. Finally, with a last look backwards at Jane, the maid left.

The doors were still open, but it was as much privacy as they were likely to get in this rigid establishment.

Mr. Whitmore took a deep breath. "I think you know that I have always held you in the highest admiration," he began. "Your success this season was truly earned. If it did not last, it is only because London society has lost the ability to appreciate honest virtues. Their refusal to accept you is their loss, not yours."

"You are too kind," Jane murmured. So news of her disgrace had reached even Mr. Whitmore. His calling on her was a mark of his true worth, showing that he cared little for the opinions of the *ton*.

Mr. Whitmore looked closely at her, then down at the tips of his boots, which appeared to hold some special fascination. "I hesitated to approach you before, but now I hope you will forgive my presumption. As you know, my wife died over a year ago. It was a happy marriage, but my one regret is that we had no children."

Jane nodded, as she wondered where this was leading.

"I have given some thought to remarriage," Mr. Whitmore continued. "Provided I could find someone suitable. I believe that I have found that someone, and I would be greatly honored if you would consent to be my wife."

"Your wife?" Jane could scarcely comprehend the meaning of his words.

"It may not be the match you were hoping for," Whitmore rushed on. "After all, with your connections you could do far better for yourself. But despite this, over the last few weeks I have seen enough to know that we would suit each other very well indeed."

It was beyond belief. After all the heartache of the last week, Jane had received an offer from a most unlikely source. She opened her mouth, then closed it when she realized she had no idea of how to respond.

Mr. Whitmore tried to forestall her possible objections. "It is true that I do not possess a title, but my name is known throughout London for fair dealing. And my fortune was not inherited, but it was honestly made through hard work. I may not be as rich as Golden Ball, but I have more than enough to provide a fine life for us. And for any children we may have."

Children! Jane blushed, as she realized the motives behind Mr. Whitmore's proposal. He was looking for a young bride who could give him heirs to carry on the business. And Jane, coming from a large family herself, must have seemed perfect for his needs. It was a sensible, blunt proposal, from a practical man. It was exactly what she had prayed for these last few days, but nonetheless she found herself hesitating.

"I am honored by your offer, sir," Jane said, feeling trapped. She needed time to think. In her agitation, she seized on his mention of her noble breeding. "I think you should know that I am not like other young ladies of the *ton.*"

"Indeed?" Mr. Whitmore asked gravely.

"It is true that my mother was a duke's daughter, but my father was a gentleman farmer. We live quite simply in Yorkshire," Jane explained, choosing her words with care. Mr. Whitmore deserved to know what he was getting into, but her family pride made her reluctant to reveal the whole of their plight. "If you are looking for a wife who can run a grand household, then I am afraid I am not the wife you need."

There. Surely he would reject her now. Jane felt a guilty sense of relief at the prospect. But Mr. Whitmore again surprised her. "I know all about your family, and their troubles," he said.

Jane gaped in astonishment. "Please do not be offended," he explained. "I wouldn't be much of a businessman if I didn't investigate thoroughly before making a commitment."

It was not the proposal of marriage that she had hoped for. There were no protestations of love, no compliments to her captivating beauty. From his words and manner, Jane gathered the impression that Mr. Whitmore had selected her as his bride with the same care he used in his business ventures. She was young and healthy and well bred. There was every reason to suppose that she would give him children to carry on his name. Jane was a logical, sensible choice.

"I am prepared to make a handsome settlement to your family on our marriage," Mr. Whitmore added. "And of course, I will see that the boys receive schooling, and that the girls are presented when it is their time." He reached over and took one of her icy hands in his own.

Jane hesitated, aware that she was on the brink of a decision that would change her life forever. The death of her father had aged her, and Jane had thought of herself as an adult ever since she took over the running of their affairs. But she could see now that she had been presumptuous. This was the moment when she would put the dreams of childhood behind her and become an adult.

Jane had one last card to play. "I have great respect for you and admiration," she said slowly. "But I can not promise anything more."

"I admire your candor," Mr. Whitmore said. "But I have no fears about that. If there is respect and admiration between the parties, then affection and even love will follow."

Jane nodded in agreement. He was right. The passionate love that the poets wrote about was hardly a good basis for a marriage. Look what had happened to her already. She had fancied herself in love with Glendale, only to find that she had given her heart to an unprincipled rogue. Mr. Whitmore was a decent and honorable man, and she should be grateful that he thought her worthy of his name.

"Then my answer is yes. I would be honored to be your wife."

Mr. Whitmore professed himself delighted. Jane allowed him to kiss her on the cheek before he took his leave, promising to return soon to discuss arrangements with Lady Barton.

After he left, Jane went to the writing desk in the corner. She began a letter to her family to inform them of her good fortune. *Dear Mama,* she began. *I have the most excellent of news. I am to be married.* A blob of ink smeared across the paper as the pen tip snapped.

"Drat this pen," Jane said, throwing the offending object across this room. She rummaged through the cubbyholes till she found another pen that met her standards. Trimming the nib carefully, she dipped the quill in ink and began to write. It was easy to describe Mr. Whitmore's kindness and thoughtfulness. She thought her family would like him. Once they got used to the idea of her marrying someone who was old enough to be her father.

But Jane's pen flowed more slowly as she attempted to describe her own happiness. It was difficult to write convincingly of something she did not feel. Her actual feelings were too hard to describe. There was relief at being able to provide for her family. And satisfaction at having spited Lady Barton by securing a husband. But mostly what she felt was akin to sadness. The last of her girlish dreams had died today. In time she would learn to find happiness in her marriage, but for now she could only think of what might have been.

A clap of thunder sounded and Glendale opened his eyes blearily, looking to find the source of the disturbance. Nothing was immediately visible, and he risked lifting his head from the satin pillowcase. This proved to be a mistake. He let his head sink back to the bed with a groan, as the demons of Hell began pounding in his skull.

An ominous *swoosh* sounded, and bright light stabbed his eyes as someone opened the drapes. "Good morning, your lordship," said his valet Timpkins cheerily. "Or rather, good afternoon."

Glendale wished passionately for a pistol. Blowing out his own brains would be a welcome relief from the aching of his head.

"Would you like your coffee in here, my lord? Or in the breakfast room?" continued Timpkins in a voice that was much too loud.

No, a pistol was definitely a bad idea. The temptation to shoot Timpkins would be irresistible.

"Quietly," Glendale rasped in a painful croak. "For the love of god, man, be quiet."

Glendale risked opening his eyes again. The light still hurt, but then his eyes became used to it and he was able to stop squinting. Slowly his brain started functioning, and he recognized the classic signs of the morning after a night of overindulgence. Just what had he been up to last night?

His brain felt fuzzy, but after a few moments thought he could remember going to the theatre. Freddie was supposed to meet him there, but after their argument, Glendale wasn't surprised that his friend never showed up. Instead he encountered Sir Peter Verney and his set. Normally Glendale steered clear of Sir Peter, but when he invited Glendale to join his friends at Vauxhall for a late supper, Glendale accepted. After Vauxhall they went to a gambling den. From there on Glendale's memories became fuzzy, although he seemed to remember something about a tavern. And a dark-haired wench named Betty.

"You're too old to behave like a fool," Glendale admonished himself.

"My lord?"

"No, not you." Glendale raised himself to a sitting position. The room rocked back and forth a few times, and then obligingly settled at a more or less even keel. "Fetch me some coffee, Timpkins."

"Would you like anything with that? Some kidneys or bacon perhaps?"

His stomach roiled at the thought. "No," Glendale said through clenched teeth. "Just coffee. And Timpkins? Do it quietly."

It took over an hour, and two pots of coffee, but with Timpkins assistance Glendale managed to turn himself into a reasonable facsimile of a gentleman. The throbbing in his head settled down to a dull ache, and he began to feel like he might live through the day.

Timpkins had brought the news of Stapleton's return, so after dressing Glendale made his way down to the study. Glendale rapped once out of politeness, then entered the study.

"Good afternoon, my lord," Stapleton said, rising to greet him.

"Stapleton, it's good to see you back. You're looking well. I take it that travel agreed with you?"

"Yes, it was an easy journey. But I must say you are not looking at all well, my lord," Stapleton observed.

Glendale lowered himself to a chair, wincing only slightly

as the chair leg scraped over the wooden floor. "It is nothing."

Stapleton arched his eyebrows in disbelief, but did not comment. "I've been going over your correspondence, and I've brought everything up to date."

Glendale nodded, impressed as usual by Stapleton's efficiency. Although, a glance at the wall clock showed that it was near three o'clock, so perhaps it wasn't that remarkable. Stapleton had probably put in a full day's work while his employer lay sleeping off the effects of his debauchery.

"And I have the information you requested regarding Miss Sedgwick," Stapleton said, reaching into his pocket and drawing out a small notebook.

"Thank you, but I am not interested in Miss Sedgwick or her family," Glendale replied stiffly.

"Indeed, my lord? But when you asked me to go to Yorkshire—"

Glendale made a chopping motion with his hand. "Things have changed since then. I know all that I need to know about Miss Sedgwick." He knew that she was a deceitful chit who only pretended friendship so she could use his influence in the *ton*. Having decided that he was too canny a bird to be brought to hand, she cast him off in search of easier game. Brooding on her betrayal, he missed Stapleton's next comment.

"What was that?" Glendale asked.

"I asked if Miss Sedgwick had confided in you?"

Glendale gave a mirthless laugh. "Yes, I suppose you could call it that."

"Well, at least the trip wasn't entirely wasted. I did see the boys back home safely." Stapleton leaned back in his chair, a faint smile playing across his face. "You know, they tried to convince me to let them down in Collinsville. Said there was no reason for me to accompany them all the way home. Naturally I refused, having your instructions otherwise."

Glendale prepared to rise, having no interest in hearing about Miss Sedgwick or her brothers, but Stapleton's next words froze him in place.

"Of course, once I was there, I understood why they were so reluctant for me to see it."

"Reluctant to let you see what?" Glendale asked.

Stapleton peered over his spectacles at his employer. "Why the cottage, of course."

Perhaps it was some lingering effect of the night's drinking, but he could make no sense at all out of Stapleton's words. "The cottage?" Glendale repeated.

"Certainly. After all, once I had seen that, there was no way to hide their circumstances, now was there?"

"No indeed," Glendale agreed, wondering when any of this was going to make sense. He rubbed one hand across his eyes, but that did nothing for his mental clarity.

"Did you know that Miss Sedgwick is one of nine children?" Stapleton asked, then continued on without waiting for an answer. "Mrs. Sedgwick was so grateful to have the boys back that she insisted I stay the night. Of course, there really isn't room in the place for a guest, but somehow they managed."

Glendale felt a faint tremor of unease as the import of Stapleton's words sank in. Surely there had been some sort of mistake. "What do you mean cottage?" Glendale asked impatiently. "Jane grew up on her father's estate in Yorkshire. She told me so herself."

Stapleton looked at him pityingly. "Well, yes, but I gather their father's death left them in rather bad straits. They've been living in the steward's cottage for years now, renting the estate out to a retired factory owner and his wife.

"The twins tried to keep quiet about it, but two days in a carriage together is not conducive to keeping secrets. Apparently their fortunes have recently taken a turn for the worse. This occasioned their journey to London. Bobby confided that he was certain that his sister would make everything right, although neither of the boys were clear on how she would do this,'' Stapleton concluded.

Glendale could feel the pieces begin to fall into place, and he wondered why he hadn't seen it sooner. ''What else did you discover?'' Glendale demanded.

Stapleton reached again for his notebook, withdrawing it from his breast pocket. It seemed an eternity while he flipped through the pages until he found the information he wanted. ''I made some discreet inquiries in Yorkshire, you understand.''

''Yes, yes, get on with it.''

Stapleton shot Glendale a sharp look, as if wondering at the source of his employer's temper. Then he continued. ''The family has been living in a precarious situation for years, but now a run of bad luck has finally caught up with them. According to the bank, the last mortgage payment is still owing. They'll have to sell everything to meet their obligations. The family will be lucky if they can keep the cottage.''

Stapleton gave a small sigh as he replaced the notebook in his pocket. ''It's a bad business all around, I'm afraid.''

Glendale agreed silently. And Stapleton knew only the half of it. Unlike his secretary, Glendale had a pretty shrewd idea of how Jane's family expected her to repair their fortunes. No doubt they were anxiously awaiting news that she had secured a wealthy husband.

No wonder she had seemed distant and troubled since the boys' visit. The weight of responsibility must have pressed heavily indeed on Jane's slender shoulders. She had to find a husband, or risk losing everything. His heart went out to her in sympathy, even as he wondered why she hadn't confided in him. She had never given so much as a hint that anything was wrong.

Or had she? Glendale thought back over their relationship. The clues had been there, but he had been too blind to see. Jane's lack of accomplishments, her hesitation about mixing with the nobility, even her tales about her family, which he could see now were always cautious never to reveal too much.

Only once had he come close to sensing the truth. Jane's distress over her brothers' unexpected appearance had awakened in him the sense that something was terribly wrong. But fool that he was, he ignored his instincts, settling for the passive course of asking Stapleton to look into things.

And the night of Mrs. Elliot's rout, when Jane had confided that she could no longer see him. What was it that she had actually said? Glendale felt a sinking sensation as he realized that she may have been trying to tell him of her plight. But he had heard only what he expected to hear.

And then he had savagely repaid her trust in him by ruining her reputation with a few thoughtless words. Even Freddie had seen Jane's goodness, but Glendale had been willfully blind. He could see that now. He had thought Julia Hanscombe a long-forgotten memory, but apparently the scars from his former fiancée's betrayal ran deep. What other explanation could there be for his actions? Jane's words had reminded him of that final scene with Miss Hanscombe, and he had leapt to the conclusion that Jane had betrayed him as well.

But there was no comparison between the two. He had been a callow youth when he courted Miss Hanscombe. She had accepted his offer of marriage, only to later spurn him in favor of a wealthy and elderly Marquis. But the fickle Miss Hanscombe had been more than willing to have Glendale as a lover, instead of a husband. Shocked by the revelation of her true character, Glendale had spurned her scandalous offer, and avoided eligible females ever since.

But whatever his past, there was no excuse for the way in which he had hurt Jane. The *ton* could be vicious when it chose, and Glendale had given them more than enough ammunition to use against her. The last few days must have been hell for her. Lord Frederick had been right to castigate him. He was no gentleman to have done such a thing to an innocent young woman.

"Is there anything else, my lord?" Stapleton asked.

Glendale looked over at his secretary. He had forgotten Stapleton's presence. "No, no," Glendale said. "I appreciate your diligence, but that will be all for now."

Even Stapleton's legendary talents couldn't resolve this situation. Glendale's public accusations had destroyed Jane's reputation, and in so doing, had robbed her of the chance to save her family by making an advantageous match. By now Jane must hate him, and with good reason. He could only hope that somehow he could find a way to make amends.

Chapter Twelve

Lady Barton took the news of the betrothal calmly. "It is unfortunate that Mr. Whitmore is in trade, of course. But after the name you have made for yourself, you are lucky that you can bring even a Cit up to scratch," she observed.

Jane gritted her teeth, forbearing to point out that the scandal was all of Lord Glendale's doing, and no fault of her own. There was no sense in breaking the uneasy truce that she and Lady Barton had established, once it had become clear that Jane would not be immediately returning to Yorkshire.

"Mr. Whitmore is received everywhere," Jane reminded Lady Barton. After all, hadn't Lady Barton herself introduced the man to Jane?

"Not quite everywhere," Lady Barton corrected her niece. "Though I own he is a good friend of Lord Barton's, which is why I always invite him when I need to make up the numbers. But Mr. Whitmore has always known his place, and knew better than to go courting any of the daughters of the *ton.* Still, in your situation, any match at all is more than you deserve."

"Mr. Whitmore is a fine man, and I am honored by his confidence in me," Jane said firmly.

Lady Barton sniffed disdainfully, but refrained from further disparaging Jane or her suitor. "One thing I must say for him, Mr. Whitmore is all dispatch. He informed me that the notices will appear in the papers tomorrow." Lady Barton's face brightened at the thought. "And once news of your engagement gets around, there is no reason why you can't resume your place in society."

What Lady Barton really meant was that *she* could return to society as well. A steady stream of invitations no longer arrived each morning at the Berkeley Square town house. Hostesses, unwilling to risk Jane's presence, had taken to dropping her aunt from the guest lists as well.

No doubt Lady Barton would have been best pleased if Jane had fled back home in disgrace. Then Lady Barton could enjoy being the center of attention, bemoaning her fate as the unwilling dupe of a scheming niece. However, since Jane showed no signs of disappearing, having Jane restored to society's good graces came a second best.

"We really must do something about the state of your wardrobe," Lady Barton said, studying her niece with a critical eye. "I will not have it said that you came to him in rags."

"But I already have more clothes than I could possibly need in a dozen lifetimes," Jane protested, unwilling to place herself further in debt to her aunt.

"Nonsense. Now that the continent is open again, travelers are bringing back the latest designs from Europe. Fashions are changing so swiftly that your frocks will soon be frightfully outmoded." Lady Barton pursed her lips thoughtfully, before adding, "In any event, you will need a dress for the wedding."

The wedding! Events were moving out of Jane's control.

Everything was happening so quickly. Why it was only yesterday that Mr. Whitmore had made his unexpected offer. Jane needed time to think, to accustom herself to the idea of being a married woman.

But there would be no leisurely engagement. Mr. Whitmore and Lady Barton had agreed between them that a wedding next month would be suitable, and Jane, mindful of her good fortune in finding any husband at all, had been unable to find any reason to object.

"Only Madame Cecile's will do," Lady Barton declared, apparently still considering the issue of a wedding dress. "And while we are there, I shall order a few of the new Parisian designs for myself."

Lady Barton's sudden interest in the state of her niece's wardrobe was now explained. From experience Jane knew that shopping with her aunt would be a tedious experience. For every article of clothing that Jane acquired, her aunt seemed to need two or three. Jane had long since concluded that Lady Barton was enjoying a subtle revenge against her husband. Lord Barton may have commanded his wife to see to Jane's presentation, but Lady Barton was making him pay dearly for his high-handedness.

The next morning dawned gray and rainy, a perfect match for Jane's spirits. Her lethargy persisted at breakfast, where even the news that the notice of her engagement was in the morning papers did little to lift her spirits. Instead the announcement seemed like a death knell, a reminder that she had chosen her path, and there was no turning back.

At the modiste's, the dressmaker was all affability. "Good morning, Lady Barton, Miss Sedgwick," Madame Cecile said brightly, rushing over to greet them. A shop assistant took their cloaks and bonnets, and Madame Cecile ushered them into her best fitting room.

Lady Barton lowered herself onto a cushioned bench, and Jane perched lightly on a nearby chair.

"Anna, bring the pattern books," Madame Cecile ordered sharply, poking her narrow face into the hallway. Then turning back to face her clients, she beamed at Jane. "I understand that felicitations are in order, Miss Sedgwick. May I be the first to wish you happy?"

"You are most kind," Jane said drily. Madame Cecile's manner was a distinct contrast to previous visits, where she had ignored Jane and lavished her attention on Lady Barton.

"You are fortunate to find such a worthy man. One hears that he is well thought of in the City," Madame Cecile added.

By which the shopkeeper meant that her future husband was known to pay his debts, Jane decided. This undoubtedly distinguished him from the careless nobility whose wives formed the bulk of Madame Cecile's clients. The dressmaker gave her another false smile, and Jane made a silent vow that once she was married she would never set foot in this shop again.

"Yes, yes," Lady Barton interjected. "We don't have all day to sit here gossiping."

"But, of course, Lady Barton. A thousand pardons," Madame Cecile said soothingly. "And how may I serve you? I have just received a set of fashion plates from Paris. The styles would look most becoming on milady. And, of course, we must discuss Miss Sedgwick's trousseau."

"There's no need for any anything elaborate," Jane protested. "The wardrobe I have will do just fine."

Madame Cecile glanced at her pityingly. "The gowns I made for you are suitable for a young woman. But once you are married, you will need a new wardrobe to match your new station in life. Is that not so, Lady Barton?"

"Most certainly," Lady Barton agreed. "Pay no attention to my niece. She is sadly lacking in knowledge of how to go on in society. It is fortunate for her that I am prepared to look out for her."

Jane bit back an angry retort, unwilling to create a public scene. Lady Barton's ideas of looking after her niece were strange indeed. Her aunt had been no help at all when the scandal broke, in fact she had helped precipitate it. Now that Jane had managed to rescue herself, Lady Barton was eager to take credit.

It was lucky for her aunt that Jane was too well bred to start a quarrel in such a public setting. That, and the bitter knowledge that without Lady Barton she would have no place to stay until the wedding.

The dressmaker took Lady Barton's advice to heart, and ignored Jane for the rest of the proceedings. Between them Lady Barton and Madame Cecile decided everything. Jane lost count of the gowns that were ordered, the fabrics that were chosen or rejected, and which styles were selected. It was a relief when Lady Barton finally declared herself satisfied.

As they left the shop, an elegant carriage pulled up to the steps. A young lady and her maid alighted, and with a sinking heart Jane recognized Miss Blake. She wondered if Miss Blake would follow the lead of the *ton* and snub her. But Miss Blake hailed her with every appearance of friendliness.

"Oh Miss Sedgwick!" Miss Blake exclaimed. Lady Barton and Jane walked down the stairs to where Miss Blake was standing on the sidewalk. "Good morning to you, Lady Barton," Miss Blake added as an afterthought.

Lady Barton inclined her head gravely but said nothing. It was left to Jane to reply. "Miss Blake, it is a pleasure to see you this morning."

"Isn't it marvelous? I was going to call on you, but Mama said I had better not, and here you are after all."

"What a coincidence," Jane observed, wondering as she always did when talking with Miss Blake, if the flighty young woman had any idea at all of what she was saying. Did Miss Blake realize that she had just insulted Jane?

"Yes, it is. I wanted to say how happy I was that everything turned out right in the end."

"It did?" Jane had no idea of what Miss Blake was referring to.

"Well yes," Miss Blake gave her a quizzical look. "After all, the notice was in the papers this morning. Even Mama said how lucky you were."

Jane clenched her fists. Why couldn't Miss Blake just congratulate her on the engagement and wish Jane happy? Why was it that everyone referred to the engagement as if it was a stroke of undeserved fortune? Jane knew she had done nothing wrong, yet the *ton* seemed determined to punish her for her imagined sins.

"It was kind of you to stop, but we really must be going," Jane said. Another moment, and she was liable to forget that she was a lady, and slap the smile off Miss Blake's vacuous countenance.

"Of course, it all is so sudden. And I never expected you to choose someone like Mr. Whitmore. He doesn't really move in our circles, does he? I can not even recall meeting him, although Mama says that I may have. And I always supposed that there was something between you and Lord Glendale," Miss Blake started, and had the grace to blush as she realized her mistake. "Er, I mean, I thought that—Well, that is of no importance now. I am late and really must take my leave." Miss Blake gave a nervous bob that was probably meant as a curtsey. "Lady Barton, Miss Sedgwick." And on that note she fled.

"An ill-bred chit if ever I saw one," Lady Barton observed. "It is a wonder that she was let out of the schoolroom."

For once Jane agreed with Lady Barton. Miss Blake's thoughtless comments had stung. So society thought that she was lucky to find any kind of husband, after Glendale had blacked her name? And she hadn't missed the implications that Mr. Whitmore would never have been considered a catch, if it wasn't for her disgrace.

A pox on Miss Blake and on the whole of society, Jane decided crossly. She wanted no part of it. It was absurd that people should praise the callous Glendale, and despise a decent and upright man like Mr. Whitmore, merely because he happened to work for a living. The more Jane saw of the so-called nobility, the more she was convinced that marrying Mr. Whitmore was the right decision. She was lucky to have found a man whose character was beyond reproach, and she would work hard to make him a good wife.

Glendale climbed the steps to Lady Barton's town house slowly, his heart full of trepidation. He had no idea of what he would say to Miss Sedgwick, but he knew that he had to see her. He owed her an apology, although he wouldn't blame her if she was unable to forgive him. For both their sakes, he hoped she would give him another chance.

The door was opened by the imperious Browning. Lady Barton's butler gave him his most haughty stare, and enquired "Yes, your lordship?"

"Is Miss Sedgwick at home?" Glendale asked.

"Miss Sedgwick is not at home," Browning replied in glacial tones. He made no move to open the door wider to permit Glendale to enter.

Glendale suddenly recalled the first time Browning had uttered those words. On that occasion Glendale had paid him no heed, inviting himself in and proceeding to interrupt Miss Sedgwick's dance lesson. Had it really been just a few short weeks ago? It seemed like Jane had been part of his life forever. And now unless he did something, she'd be gone from him for good.

"And Lady Barton?"

"Lady Barton is also not at home. Would your lordship care to leave a card?"

Leave a card as if he were some casual acquaintance? Browning had never been friendly, but now he was treating Glendale with all the warmth reserved for upstart mushrooms and counter-jumpers.

"No," Glendale said shortly. But after a moment he reconsidered. Reaching into his coat pocket he pulled out his silver card case. "Tell Miss Sedgwick that I must speak with her," Glendale said, extracting a card from the case.

"I will see that she is so informed," Browning said. With a dignified nod he shut the door in Glendale's face.

Glendale stood there for a moment, staring foolishly at the closed door. The butler had made him feel like a recalcitrant schoolboy. But his attitude had answered one question at least. There was no question of whom Browning felt responsible for the scandal that had enveloped the occupants of 19 Berkeley Square.

Glendale called back later, and was rebuffed by a footman. The footman claimed no knowledge of the ladies' whereabouts, but the sight of a golden guinea greatly improved his memory, to the point where he was able to recall that they had recently departed on a shopping expedition. The news cheered Glendale. Perhaps Miss Sedgwick had truly not been at home when he first called.

Glendale waited till five o'clock before he tried again. At this hour the ladies were certain to have returned home. And according to the talkative footman, they were planning to dine at home, so there was no chance that he would miss them.

The first setback to his plans occurred when the door was opened by the imperious Browning, instead of the covetous young James. "Miss Sedgwick is not at home," Browning said, before Glendale had a chance to state his errand.

"Indeed?"

"Miss Sedgwick has informed me that she is not at home, that she will *never* be at home to your lordship." Browning's eyes glimmered with satisfaction as he delivered this set-down. "However, Lady Barton has no objections to your company, if you should care to step inside."

Blast! He had no interest in talking to his uncle's wife. It was Lady Barton's fault that they were in this mess in the first place. If she hadn't held that dinner party, throwing an unprepared Jane to the wolves as it were, then he and Freddie would never have dreamed up that idiotic wager. Glendale knew he was being irrational, but there was no help for it.

But what to do now? The idea of breaking the door down and forcing his way in held a certain appeal, even as he dismissed the idea as impractical. True, he could force his way in to see Jane, but he had no way of making her listen to him. What he needed was an intermediary. Lady Barton came to mind, but he was unwilling to ask Lady Barton to intercede for him.

Who was there in London that Jane would trust? No name came to mind. Except for himself and Lord Frederick, she hadn't seemed especially close to anyone. But the thought of Freddie gave him an idea. Perhaps Freddie could help. After all, he had championed Jane's cause the last time they met, so surely he would be willing to lend his assistance. And Freddie had the distinct advantage of having three sisters in London this season. If a female accomplice was required, they would not have to look far. Crossing to the writing table Glendale dashed off a quick note, then rang the bell to summon a footman.

"See to it that this message is delivered to Lord Frederick at once," Glendale instructed.

"Yes, my lord," the footman replied.

"You're to put it in his hands, and no one else's," Glendale continued. "I don't care if it takes all day and night. Don't come back until you find him."

"As you wish, my lord."

The footman eyed him speculatively, but when no further instructions were forthcoming, he gave a quick bow and went off on his errand.

The footman returned in the early evening, his mission accomplished, but it was breakfast time the next morning before Lord Frederick saw fit to respond to Glendale's hastily scrawled summons.

"Lord Frederick is here. Shall I show him in, my lord?" Fisk enquired.

"Never mind, I'll show myself in," Freddie said, stepping around Fisk and entering the morning room. "Be a good chap and bring me some coffee," Freddie added, as he seated himself at the opposite end of the table from Glendale.

The young footman gave Glendale a nervous look, uncertain of his master's temper.

"Fetch us both some coffee, if you would," Glendale instructed. "I've already breakfasted, but would you care for something?"

"No, no," Freddie shuddered at the notion. "It is much too early to be thinking about food. Just coffee."

Glendale watched impatiently as Freddie made a ritual out of adding cream and sugar in exact portions, sipped critically, then put the cup down to add more sugar. Finally Freddie pronounced himself satisfied, and the hovering footman left.

"Thank you for coming by," Glendale began.

"How could I not? After receiving your elegant apology," Freddie responded.

"Apology? What apology?" The tersely worded note had merely said that Glendale needed to see Freddie on a matter of importance.

"The one that you are about to make me." The playfulness left Freddie's expression, and he lowered the cup into the saucer. "I am waiting."

Glendale should have known that his old friend wasn't going to make this easy for him. "Very well. I apologize. I was a fool. A cork-brained sapskull. A veritable out-and-outer. No gentleman would have acted as I did. I deserve to be drawn and quartered for my crimes. I—"

"That's enough," Freddie interjected. "After all, I was part of this harebrained wager."

"Yes, but you weren't the one who made it common knowledge."

It was the unvarnished truth. There was nothing Freddie could say that would alter the circumstances. Instead he chose to change the subject. "So when did you come to your senses, and what are you going to do about it?"

Glendale paused, uncertain of how much to reveal to Lord Frederick. "I discovered that Miss Sedgwick's background isn't quite what we thought it was."

"Don't try and tell me that she's illegitimate, or that her mother eloped with a stable boy, and that is why the family is stuck in Yorkshire."

"No, it isn't like that. But didn't you think it odd that Miss Sedgwick was so ill-prepared for the Season?"

"Of course I did. We both did. That's why we made that silly wager and got ourselves into this coil," Freddie said impatiently.

So much for his attempts to hint at the truth. "There's a simple explanation. When Jane's father died he left the family in a rather bad way. They've barely been getting by for the last few years. There was no money for any luxuries. No governess, no schooling for her brothers, no fancy ball gowns or dancing masters. They're practically in Dun Territory."

Freddie whistled soundlessly at this revelation. "So that's why." A thought seemed to strike him. "Does Lady Barton know?"

"She must," Glendale said drily. "But there's some quarrel there, and she's never offered to help. If it wasn't for my uncle insisting that she do right by her family, Jane would still be stuck in the country.''

And he would never have met her. Would never have known that someone as special as Jane existed. As much as he regretted his actions, Glendale still felt fortunate to have encountered her.

''So what does this have to do with the other night?'' Freddie persisted, breaking into Glendale's train of thought.

''Well, things have gotten rather worse for the family. It looks like they're about to lose everything. Jane tried to confide in me the other night, but I misunderstood.'' It was painful to remember the encounter. Jane's worried eyes, the hesitancy in her speech, her shock when he rebuffed her; how different everything appeared now that he knew the truth. ''She told me that she couldn't afford to wait any longer to make a match. I took her words amiss, and the rest you know.''

There. It was out. Glendale felt better for having finally confessed. ''I don't know what I was thinking,'' he added.

Freddie had remained silent as the tale unfolded, appearing engrossed in tracking the patterns of the linen tablecloth with his spoon. Now he looked directly at Glendale. ''Yes, you do. You were thinking of that poisonous bitch Julia Hanscombe.''

Glendale flinched. It had been years since anyone had dared mention her name in his presence. Even now, the memory of his former fiancée still stung.

''Perhaps.''

''Perhaps nothing. But how could you make such a mistake? Jane is nothing like Miss Hanscombe.''

True. Julia Hanscombe had accepted Glendale's offer of marriage with a becoming show of shyness. Her father pleaded for a long engagement, citing the youth of both parties. Six months after the engagement she had shown no such shyness when she threw Glendale over for a much wealthier nobleman. A Marquess, no less, who unlike Glendale had already inherited his title. An elderly Marquess to boot, one who left her a gay widow not too many years later.

Julia Hanscombe's betrayal had cut deeply. At the time Glendale had believed himself in love with her, although now, years later, he could see that it had been a mere infatuation. Glendale had been barely twenty at the time, too young and inexperienced to know his own heart.

He had thought himself long over the fickle Miss Hanscombe. But all it had taken was a few misspoken words from Jane to bring back the pain. And the innocent Jane had taken the brunt of his anger.

"I won't argue with you," Glendale said. "What's done is done. The point is, how do I make amends?"

"Have you talked with Miss Sedgwick?"

Glendale laughed mirthlessly. "Talked with her? I can't even see her. I called yesterday and was told in no uncertain terms that she was unwilling to see me. Then or ever."

"Hmm," Freddie said thoughtfully. "That does make it tricky. What about her aunt? Surely if you explain to Lady Barton that you intend to apologize, she'll insist on Jane seeing you."

"You may be right," Glendale said reluctantly. If Lady Barton was his only chance, then he would overcome his distaste for her. "But is an apology really enough? I'm afraid I damaged Jane's reputation rather badly."

"What else can you do?"

Glendale paused, letting silence fill the room. After a few moments, he said, "I could always offer to marry her," giving voice to the thought that had been at the back of his mind.

Freddie laughed. "That's a good idea. But I think her intended might object. And having two fiancés would really put Miss Sedgwick beyond the pale."

"Fiancé?" Glendale asked. It couldn't be true. She was his. Freddie must be mistaken.

Freddie studied him with a keen eye. "You didn't know? It was in the papers yesterday. Jane's gotten herself engaged to that Cit. Whitehead or Whitstone, or whatever his name was."

"Whitmore. James Whitmore," Glendale corrected absently. Jane, engaged? Promised to another man? In all his thoughts he had never considered this possibility. He felt robbed, as if someone had stolen something precious from him. Something that he only noticed when it was gone.

"Well, have you decided what you're going to do?" Freddie asked.

"No. But I am certain I will think of something." He knew one thing. Jane wasn't in love with Mr. Whitmore. She couldn't be. She was sacrificing herself for the sake of her family.

It was Glendale's fault that she had come to this, and it was up to him to find a way to extricate her from this mess. He owed it to her. And to himself, for he wasn't about to give her up without a fight.

Chapter Thirteen

"I've found it!" Sally held up the offending glove as she emerged triumphantly from the depths of the wardrobe. "Here now, put this on quick. You don't want to be late, Miss Jane."

"There is more than enough time. The guests aren't expected for nearly an hour," Jane replied. She drew on the satin gloves, then rose from her chair. Walking over to the cheval mirror she examined her appearance with a critical eye. The lace gown was lovely, but even Madame Cecile's best work couldn't disguise Jane's unfashionable height. And the low décolletage would draw unwanted attention to the generous bosom that nature had seen fit to endow her with.

"It's a shame that your necklace is still at the jeweler's," Sally commented. "The pearls would be just the thing with that."

Jane felt herself blushing, and one hand flew up to her bare neck. "I was tired of them anyway," Jane prevaricated.

"If you say so, miss."

Jane turned away, unable to meet the maid's knowing gaze. When Sally first noticed that the pearls were missing, Jane had hastily concocted the story of a broken clasp, and a trip to the jeweler's to have them repaired. But that was two weeks ago, and Sally was getting suspicious.

A knock sounded at the door, saving Jane from having to embroider further on the tale. Sally walked through the dressing room to the bedroom and opened the hallway door. Through the door, Jane caught a glimpse of one of the household's many footmen.

"Sally, tell Miss Sedgwick that Lady Barton would like to see her in the drawing room," the footman said, loudly enough for Jane to hear him.

"I'll tell her," Sally said. "And it's Miss Penny to you, you cloth-head." With a toss of her head, she shut the door firmly in the footman's face.

Sally was still muttering when she returned to the dressing room. "Who does he think he is anyway? I'm not one of the housemaids who goes moony whenever he smiles at 'em."

It was hard not to smile at Sally's indignation. Sally relished her promotion to the exalted position of lady's maid, and was quick to set down anyone who failed to recognize her new status.

Jane's smile quickly faded however, as she left the room and descended to the first floor. She couldn't help remembering the two previous occasions when Lady Barton had entertained. Jane winced at the remembrance of that disastrous first dinner party. It hurt to remember how naive she had been.

Even her memories of her come-out ball, which had once seemed so grand and glorious, were now tainted. For her memories of the evening were wrapped up with memories of Lord Glendale, and his subsequent betrayal.

Jane paused outside the drawing room, taking time to calm her jangling nerves. She had nothing to fear tonight.

There would be some uncomfortable moments, but the guests had been carefully chosen by Lady Barton. They might come out of curiosity, but they could be counted on to behave civilly.

When Jane entered the room, she discovered Lady Barton sitting in her favorite chair by the fire.

"Good evening, Lady Barton," Jane said, crossing the room to greet her aunt. "I trust you are well?"

"Tolerable," Lady Barton said.

Jane bent down to kiss her aunt's withered cheek. As she straightened back up, Jane saw a gentleman standing in the shadows near the window. He looked familiar, but it couldn't be, could it?

"Matthew?" Jane intended to shout, but the words came out in a whisper instead.

"Now Cornelia, Lord Glendale is here to make his apologies."

How dare they trick her in this way! Jane knew that Glendale had been trying to see her for the last week, and it had given her great pleasure to refuse him admittance.

"I have no intention of listening to anything he has to say," Jane declared.

Lady Barton reached up and grasped Jane's arm to keep her from leaving. Lady Barton's grip was surprisingly strong for a woman of her age. "Yes, you will, because I say so. It is the least that you can do, considering all I have done for you."

There was no missing the implied threat in Lady Barton's words. Until her marriage, Jane was still dependent on her aunt's generosity.

"Very well," Jane said. She would listen, but there was nothing Glendale could say that would change her opinion of him.

Lady Barton released her grip on Jane's arm, and then heaved her bulk out of the chair. Her parting words were addressed to Glendale. "You have five minutes. And I am leaving the door open."

Jane turned her back on Glendale and stared at the fire, as if fascinated by the flickering coals. She heard Glendale's footsteps as he crossed the room, but she refused to give him the satisfaction of acknowledging his presence. He finally stopped a few feet away from her.

"Jane, I am so terribly sorry," he said. "I do not expect that you can ever forgive me." His voice was quiet, colored by some strong emotion.

His words startled her. This was not the practiced, empty apology that she had somehow expected. Glendale sounded as if he meant what he was saying.

Jane turned around and met his gaze steadily. "You are correct, my lord. What you did was unforgivable."

She had the satisfaction of seeing Glendale flinch. He opened his mouth to say something, and then closed it, as if at a loss for words. This was another first. The glib, witty Glendale with nothing to say. In the ensuing silence, Jane took the opportunity to study him. He looked different than she remembered. His face was thinner and paler than she recalled, and there were new lines around his eyes.

"I never meant for you to be hurt," Glendale explained.

"Is that so? You thought I wouldn't mind learning that I was merely the subject of a wager? You deceived me, and feigned friendship, and this was supposed to make me happy? While all the time, you were laughing at my naiveté." Jane's anger mounted as she relived the memory of his betrayal. The pain she felt was physical, a dull ache in her chest. "How, pray tell, was I not supposed to be hurt by this?"

"The wager was a drunken bit of foolishness, between myself and Freddie. We didn't—that is, I didn't know you then. Anyone could see that you weren't ready for London.

So we wagered about whether or not you would stick it out. It wasn't very noble of us, but we didn't see the harm."

An impartial observer might have conceded this point. Jane had been woefully unprepared for London society. And gentlemen wagered all the time, over matters as weighty as the war with Napoleon, to things as trivial as a falling raindrop.

But conceding that the wager was harmless did not excuse his subsequent behaviour. "And afterwards?"

Glendale ran one hand through his hair, betraying his nervousness. "The more time I spent with you, the more I wanted to get to know you. To be with you. I had never met anyone like you before, never felt for them the way I did for you." He took a deep breath before continuing. "To tell the truth, I had forgotten all about the wager, until that night."

"Then why did you say the things you did? What did I ever do to you, that you should treat me so?" Jane demanded, giving voice to the pain that had troubled her since his betrayal. To her mortification, her voice broke on the last words.

Glendale stepped closer, raising his arms as if to reach for her. Jane took a hasty step backwards and he halted his advance. She didn't know whether or not to be relieved. She longed for the comfort of his embrace, yet at the same time she felt as if she would shatter into a thousand pieces if he touched her.

"That night, when you asked for my advice, I misunderstood you. I heard what I expected to hear. What I'd heard before." Glendale broke eye contact and began to pace, as if unable to keep still. "Did you know that I was engaged once?" he said, so quietly that she had to strain to hear his words.

He looked over, and Jane shook her head.

"Well, it was a long time ago. Her name was Julia Hanscombe, and she was the most sought-after catch of the

Season. I thought myself lucky when she accepted my suit." Glendale grimaced at some memory. "The signs were all there, but I couldn't see them. She was lively and charming, and loved nothing better than being the center of attention."

Unwillingly Jane felt herself drawn to the story. Even her anger with Glendale couldn't keep her from sensing the pain behind his words.

"And then she came to me, and said she couldn't marry me after all. There was this Marquess, you see. And he was elderly, and very, very wealthy. And he was willing to buy her all the baubles she desired. As for me, well, my father was still alive, and she decided she had no wish to wait for her title."

"It sounds like you had a lucky escape," Jane said.

He gave a short bark of laughter. "Indeed. But I didn't think so at the time. I thought I loved her, and couldn't understand how she could betray me."

Betrayal. Jane could sympathize with the young Glendale. She knew the pain of being betrayed by love. She reminded herself that she, not Glendale, was the injured party. Whatever had happened in the past, it could not excuse his actions. "I am sorry, but—"

Glendale made a brusque gesture, cutting her off. "I didn't tell you this to gain your sympathy. But you needed to hear it, to understand what happened the other night. In all these years, I've never considered offering for another woman. Never felt I could trust a woman enough to tie myself to her like that. Then I met you. And you were so different from everyone else. So honest. So caring. You said what you thought, without all the layers of pretense."

He paused, but Jane could think of nothing to say. Her mind was whirling as she considered his revelations. Why hadn't she ever wondered about this before? Glendale's single state was a matter of great comment in the *ton,* given his title and responsibilities. She should have known that there was more to his refusal to consider marriage than a simple unwillingness to settle down.

"And then that night," Glendale said. "You came to me for advice."

Jane remembered that night. Remembered how anxious and nervous she had been. Remembered, too, how she had made a botch of explaining her situation. "And I told you that I needed to marry for money," Jane said, finally breaking the silence.

"Yes. And it seemed suddenly that I had misjudged you all along. My pride was hurt, and I acted on impulse. If Freddie hadn't been there, who knows what would have happened? But he was convenient, and I spoke of the wager, knowing that my words would be repeated."

"I see," Jane said. "I understand, even if I find it difficult to forgive." She understood all too well. Glendale had imagined himself betrayed for the second time, and had taken his revenge on her. It didn't matter that she was the innocent victim of his rage. He had been hurt, and he had lashed out, intending to hurt her in return.

Before the last few weeks, Jane would have never understood how passionate emotion could drive someone to such an act. But now she knew differently. In the white hot heat of her own anger, she might have done or said anything if she could have been certain of wounding Glendale.

But understanding what had happened did not change the past. Even the most eloquent of apologies could not erase the events of the last two weeks. Glendale's words had come perilously close to a declaration of love, but it was much too late for that.

"Can you forgive me?" he asked. "I want to make amends."

Jane made the mistake of looking into his eyes. There was an equal mixture of hope and sadness in his expression.

She longed to tell him that she forgave him, that everything could be as it was before. But that was impossible now.

"Well, I forgave Freddie, so I suppose I must forgive you as well," Jane said with a brittle laugh.

"And will you let me requite my wrongs?"

"I am afraid it is too late for that. Many things have changed. I am to marry Mr. Whitmore, you know," Jane said, wondering what his reaction would be.

"Yes, I know," Glendale replied. "Allow me to wish you happy."

Jane waited, half-hoping that he would say something else. That he would say it was not too late for her to change her mind. If he cared for her at all, how could he take so calmly the news that she was to marry another? Or was his silence an acknowledgment that she had irrevocably committed herself to Mr. Whitmore?

Glendale reached inside his coat, and withdrew a small, velvet-covered box. "I brought you a gift," he said. Jane made no move to take it, so he lifted her right hand, and placed the box in her palm.

Her hand tingled where he touched it, unnerving her. It was a reminder that no other man had ever made her feel this way. "I cannot accept this," Jane said, for form's sake.

"But you must," Glendale replied. Then, with a trace of impatience, he added, "Open it at least, before you decide."

It could do no harm to look. She lifted the lid of the box, then gasped in wonder. Inside, nestled on white satin, lay a familiar string of pearls, set in the antique style of her grandmother's time. How had he known? How had he found them?

"I never thought to see these again, Matthew," she said.

Glendale smiled, seemingly pleased by her happiness. "They are lovely yes, but they will look more beautiful on you." Reaching into the box, he withdrew the necklace.

The pearls glistened in the light. Before she could stop him, he fastened the string around her throat. She trembled as his fingers brushed her neck and the sensitive hollow of her throat, as he deftly arranged the necklace. "There now, that's better," he said.

No, this was not better. His fingers were gone, but she could still feel the tingling where he had touched her. She wanted him to touch her again, to be swept up in his embrace. What kind of wanton was she, to be thinking such things when she was engaged to another?

She should never have agreed to talk with him. Should never have forgiven him. Her anger would have shielded her from this attraction. Now what was she to do?

Glendale wanted to spend more time with Jane, but the arrival of the first of the guests put an end to their tête-à-tête. He was on his best behavior, even managing to congratulate James Whitmore on the engagement with seeming goodwill. The guests were surprised at his presence, but no one was gauche enough to mention the rift. On the contrary, the show of family solidarity would give the rumormongers something else to talk about.

As guests of honor, Jane and Mr. Whitmore were seated together, on the opposite side of the table from his own place. Glendale studied her, but could find no clue as to her emotions. She seemed at ease, and conversed pleasantly enough with her dinner partners.

But was she happy? Was this match what she truly wanted? Glendale had promised Freddie that he would do nothing rash. Having acted hastily once, Glendale was resolved to be more cautious this time. To ascertain Jane's feelings before he acted. There was no sense in saving a woman who did not want to be saved.

It seemed incredible that he had once thought Jane the easiest of persons to read. Her emotions had shown plainly on her face. Happiness, excitement, affection, and trepidation had shone freely for all to see. But not tonight. Jane had learned another of the bitter lessons that life in London taught. She had learned the cost of sharing her feelings, and now hid behind a mask of politeness. It was a lesson she should never have had to learn.

Glendale was still frustrated by the time dinner was over. The ladies rose to retire, and as he watched Jane disappear, he realized he was no closer to discerning her feelings than he had been before this night. He had no notion of what to do next. Should he leave matters as they were? Glendale toyed absently with his glass of port, taking no part in the conversation around him.

"Didn't think to see you here," Lord David Cartland said, nudging Glendale to get his attention. The young lord's face was flushed with the amount of port he had consumed.

Glendale was in no mood for conversation with drunken lordlings. "Indeed," he said in his chilliest voice, hoping the young puppy would take the hint.

But Lord Cartland was too far gone to notice. "I said," he repeatedly loudly, as if Glendale might be deaf, "Didn't 'spect to shee—to see you here. After what you said about the girl. Calling her a fortune hunter and all."

Cartland's loud words had attracted the attention of the others. The room grew still. Glendale looked over at Mr. Whitmore, whose set expression indicated that he, too, had heard the remark.

"You are mistaken," Glendale said, fixing Cartland with an icy stare.

"But I was there. I heard—"

"You are mistaken," Glendale repeated. "I trust you will not make such a mistake again. It might be taken as a slur against my honor."

Drunk as he was, young Cartland did not miss the veiled threat. As Glendale had suspected, the young puppy had no stomach for facing a challenge from an opponent with Glendale's reputation. "Of course," Cartland mumbled, "You are right. Don't know what I heard. It must have been someone else, something else. Or maybe I wasn't even there . . ." His voice trailed off into silence.

Glendale turned his shoulder to Cartland, satisfied that Cartland had been put in his place. And the news of his threat to challenge Cartland would travel swiftly throughout the *ton.* Knowing that Glendale was prepared to defend Jane's honor would give society pause. It wasn't much to do for her, but it was a beginning.

Chapter Fourteen

The morning after the dinner party, Mr. Whitmore called at Berkeley Square. Through a stroke of good luck, Lady Barton was engaged, leaving Jane to receive Mr. Whitmore. She greeted him warmly, pleased that they would have a chance to talk privately. Well, almost privately. The ever-watchful Sally, busy with some bit of mending, did not really count.

Jane had seen little of her fiancé since the engagement was announced. In many ways Mr. Whitmore was still a stranger to her, yet they would be wed in less than a month. Jane tried not to dwell on that thought, and instead concentrate on learning all she could about her future husband.

She rang for refreshments, and listened to Mr. Whitmore's impressions of last night's dinner. When the cart arrived, she expertly poured coffee for Mr. Whitmore, and then tea for herself.

"I must admit, I was surprised to see Lord Glendale in attendance," Mr. Whitmore said blandly.

Jane gazed sharply at him, but Mr. Whitmore appeared

disinterested. "Yes, well, he is family, and it would have looked odd not to invite him," she replied.

"Even after the way he treated you?"

"It was a misunderstanding," Jane said firmly. "Lord Glendale has made his apologies, and that is the end of the matter."

"Indeed," Mr. Whitmore observed, but to her relief he did not press the matter further. There was a long moment of silence.

Glendale was a topic best left unexplored. Jane did not want to know what Mr. Whitmore thought of Glendale, or of her own relationship with him. She seized eagerly on another topic to divert his thoughts. "I had a letter from my mother the other day. She and the twins will be arriving shortly, in plenty of time for the wedding."

The rest of her brothers and sisters would be staying at home. When Lady Barton and Mr. Whitmore had made the wedding plans, it had been decided that a quiet London wedding would be best. There was no reason for Mr. Whitmore to travel to the wilds of Yorkshire, just so Jane's family could see her wed. And Lady Barton, while grudgingly willing to give houseroom to her sister and the two oldest boys, would extend her hospitality no farther.

Lady Barton would have excluded even the twins, but Jane insisted that her brothers would be the ones to walk her down the aisle. Her mother had written that Bobby and Dick were pleased to be coming to London, but not at all agreeable to the notion of dressing in their Sunday best.

"I trust your family is well?"

"Yes, all quite well."

"Good." Mr. Whitmore stretched his legs out and leaned back in the chair. "I wrote to your family's man of business, and instructed him to see that the Manor Hall is put to rights. With luck, everything should be finished by the time your mother is to return home."

"You are much too kind," Jane said. She meant it sincerely, but it seemed that she was always thanking Mr. Whitmore for one thing or another. Her betrothed had redeemed the mortgages on the farmland and Manor Hall, and sent money to Mr. Timerson to settle the rest of their debts. A generous settlement was to be made on her family once they were married. At times she felt weighed down by the burden of gratitude. "It will be wonderful to see the old Manor restored again."

"What? Oh yes, I suppose we will see it sometime," Mr. Whitmore said. "Yorkshire is a long journey, but perhaps we could go for a visit someday." He frowned thoughtfully as he consulted some mental calendar. "Not this summer, though. Business will be much too busy. And of course winter is no time to travel. But by next summer things may be quieter."

Jane's chest constricted, as the import of his words sank in. Not to see her family for a year or more? Why little Michael would be grown without recognition! Certain that her distress must show on her face, she turned away from Mr. Whitmore and busied herself with the tea tray.

Jane reminded herself that Mr. Whitmore was a good man. A kind man. It wasn't his fault that his business affairs left him little time for socializing or visiting. Surely they would be able to work out some kind of compromise. "Whatever you say," Jane finally replied. "Although if I am absent for too long, my family is liable to come looking for me."

Her voice must have betrayed her unhappiness, for Mr. Whitmore reached over and patted her hand. "My dear, you know that they will always be welcome. And you may visit them whenever you please, although I will seldom be free to accompany you."

Jane gave him a determinedly bright smile. "I understand," she said. "Please forgive my moodiness. It is natural that I will miss my family, but then of course I will have you."

But Mr. Whitmore would make a poor replacement for her boisterous and loving family. She had already seen for herself how little time her future husband had to spend with her. There was no reason to expect he would change after the marriage. He had even mentioned that his agent was looking into country properties, within a few hours of London. Somewhere quiet, since the City was no place to raise children. Their children. But Jane was beginning to fear that she would be expected to raise them on her own.

Freddie was late as usual, blast his eyes. Glendale pulled out his pocket watch and flipped the cover open. It must be broken, for it showed only two minutes had passed since the last time he checked. Glendale held the watch up to his ear, but the steady ticking didn't reassure him. Perhaps the watch had stopped and only just started again.

Glendale strode across the foyer and threw open the door to the front parlor. The door handle made a satisfying crack as it struck the wall. He leaned in and glanced at the ornate clock on the mantelpiece. Time itself must have ceased, for the treacherous clock confirmed the testimony of his watch.

Glendale resumed his pacing. After a brief pause, the young footman James went over and closed the parlor door, careful to stay out of Glendale's path.

A knock sounded at the front door. James reached it first, with an impressive show of speed, and opened the door to reveal the long-awaited Lord Frederick.

Glendale, who had been wearing his cape for the last half hour, brushed by the footman. He would have forgotten his hat and gloves if James hadn't thrust them into his hands. "You're late, Freddie," was his greeting.

"Nonsense," Freddie said cheerfully. At Glendale's

scowl he amended his words. "Well, maybe a little, but considering that I brought Priscilla, I think I did quite well. You know how females are. Never satisfied with how they look, so they're never ready on time."

Glendale could name at least one woman who wouldn't have kept him waiting. But Jane had little in common with the flighty Priscilla.

Glendale followed Freddie down to the carriage. "I see you still have the grays," he said, referring to the matched horses that were harnessed to the carriage.

"Yes, aren't they something?" Freddie beamed proudly.

"Indeed." They were definitely a sight to turn heads. The harness was all gleaming silver and black leather, matching the trim on Freddie's newest carriage. Silver ribbons were elaborately braided in the horses' manes and tails. Even the horses' hooves had been painted black. Glendale hoped that Freddie was paying his stable lads well for all the extra work.

Freddie paused by the horses' heads, on the pretext of showing off the matched pair. "Now, before you get in the carriage, tell me that you remember your promise."

"What promise?" Glendale asked, with feigned innocence.

The color mounted in Freddie's cheeks. "Oh, no, you're not wiggling out of this. You promised to escort Priscilla tonight."

"And you doubt my word?"

"Of course not. It's just that I know you," Freddie replied, with his own peculiar brand of logic. "So I am warning you now. Miss Sedgwick is to be my companion for the evening. After all, a man with my reputation can't be seen taking his sister around. Makes it look like I've nothing better to do."

Glendale widened his eyes. "Nothing could be simpler. You will escort Miss Sedgwick, and I will squire your sister.

Now may we get in the carriage? Jane will be wondering where we have disappeared to."

Freddie looked at him sharply. "Why don't I trust you?" But he made no further protest and motioned for the groom, who opened the carriage door.

The excursion to the Opera was Glendale's idea. Ostensibly, Freddie would be escorting Miss Sedgwick, and Glendale would be Priscilla's escort. Glendale had convinced his friend to go along with the plan, arguing that their appearing in such a public setting would show the *ton* that they were all on good terms, and help defuse the gossip.

It was a good reason. It just wasn't the only reason. Having Freddie offer the invitation ensured that Jane wouldn't refuse. But Glendale had no intention of allowing Freddie to monopolize Jane for the evening. When they reached the Opera House, Glendale made his move.

He allowed Freddie and Jane to proceed them into the box, which Freddie's mother had lent for the occasion. There were four gilt chairs, arranged in two pairs. Freddie seated Jane in the front, and then sat himself next to her.

Glendale seated Priscilla and himself. Then he glanced at his companion, as if struck by a sudden thought. "No, this will never do. Miss Pennington, I never realized how charmingly petite you are."

Miss Pennington blushed and giggled on cue.

"And I know how much you were looking forward to seeing this production. Why don't you change places with Miss Sedgwick? She is so much taller, she will be able to see perfectly well from the back."

The couple in front turned to stare at them. The look on Freddie's face was priceless. Priscilla rose from her seat, and Jane stood up as well. In a trice the ladies had exchanged places. Freddie stood up as well, but Glendale remained seated.

"I believe you are in my chair," Freddie said stiffly.

Glendale leaned back in the chair, stretching his legs

out in front of him, effectively blocking Freddie's path. "Well, actually I am in your mother's chair. We all are. And wasn't it kind of her to lend them to us? Now, be a good chap and sit down. Can't you see they are about to start?"

Freddie sat down, muttering about treacherous snakes and ungrateful cads.

"That was a shabby trick you played on Lord Frederick," Jane said softly.

"Yes, it was," Glendale agreed. "I hope you don't object." If Jane was upset, he was prepared to exchange places with Freddie. But he hoped she wouldn't mind the change of escorts.

"No, I prefer it back here. When one is in the front of the box, you are conscious of the eyes that are upon you. Here it is easier to pretend that no one is looking at you."

Well, at least she hadn't objected to his company. "If you are uncomfortable, we can leave. I—that is, Freddie—invited you because I remembered how much you enjoyed your earlier visit."

"It was very kind of Lord Frederick to invite me," Jane replied, giving an ironic stress to Lord Frederick's name. "I hate to impose on Lady Barton, and Mr. Whitmore has scant time for socializing these days." An expression of sadness passed over her face, so fleeting that a lesser observer might have missed it.

Her expression confirmed his feeling that Jane was not happy in her engagement. But the music had started, and there was no chance to pursue his suspicions. Glendale could hardly conduct a private conversation with Jane in the raised voices that were necessary to be heard over the operatic arias.

Jane gave her full attention to the unfolding drama, seeming absorbed by Mozart's tale of star-crossed lovers. Glendale had winced when he realized that the company was performing *The Magic Flute.* Such romantic fare was hardly appropriate, given their situation.

Glendale crossed his legs, swinging one foot back and forth. Nothing was turning out as he had hoped. There had been no chance for private conversation with Miss Sedgwick. During the interval between acts, their box had rapidly filled with acquaintances curious to behold the sight of Jane and Glendale on such apparent good terms.

And now the second half had begun. And he was no further towards his goal than he had been two hours earlier. On stage, the stout diva who played the Princess was singing her lungs out, proclaiming her love for Tamino. But Tamino, sworn to silence, did not respond. Glendale glanced over at Jane, to see what she thought of the hapless lovers.

A single tear rolled down her creamy white cheek. And then it was joined by another. Clearly Jane could feel all too well the anguish of the lovers. She fumbled for her reticule. Glendale reached into his coat and withdrew a linen handkerchief.

"Let me," he said, leaning over towards her. With infinite tenderness he wiped her swollen eyes. His gentleness proved her undoing. Jane turned her face towards him.

"It's so unfair," she said, her voice thick with tears. He could not tell whether she meant the plot of the opera, her own situation, or life itself. He suspected that she herself was not sure what she meant. "Why can't people just be happy?" With those words she broke down into tears.

Glendale gathered Jane to his chest, her tears wilting his cravat. "There now," he said, stroking her dark hair. "Everything will be all right."

"How can it be? I've ruined everything," Jane sobbed.

Her words were loud enough to catch the attention of the pair in front. Freddie's back went rigid, but like a true gentleman he continued to look straight ahead. Priscilla, however, gave in to her youthful curiosity and turned around to stare at Jane. With a firm hand, Freddie reached over and grasped his sister's chin, turning her gaze back to the stage where it belonged.

It was time that they settled this. Glendale reached forward and tapped Frederick on the shoulder. When Freddie turned around, Glendale informed him, "Miss Sedgwick is not feeling well. I am taking her home."

Freddie nodded. "Take my carriage. Prissy and I can take a hackney."

"Thank you," Glendale said, grateful for his friend's understanding. Freddie might make a fuss over trifles, but he was completely reliable in a crunch.

Glendale bundled Jane into her cloak and escorted her down the stairs and out into the street. She had stopped crying, but said little until they were inside the carriage.

"Thank you," Jane said. "I don't know what came over me."

Jane slid over to the far end of the bench, placing as much distance as she could between them. Glendale moved over next to her, and wrapped one arm around her shoulders. Jane stiffened, but did not pull away. She fit perfectly against him, her head leaning against his shoulders as if she belonged there, by his side.

"We can not go on like this. You can not keep pretending that everything is fine," he stated.

"I don't know what you mean," Jane said hesitantly.

He could see that she was still upset. A gentleman wouldn't press her in her condition, but time was running out. And he might never have a better opportunity than now.

"You know what I mean," Glendale retorted. "You're not the type to fall to pieces over a silly romantic opera. Not unless something else is bothering you. Why can't you admit that you've made a mistake? You were never meant to marry Mr. Whitmore."

"Mr. Whitmore is a good man."

"Yes, but do you love him?" There was no answer. Jane would not look at him. How dare she try to pretend, to him of all people? Glendale tightened his arm around her, angrily demanding, "Do you love him?"

"No!" Jane shouted. Then she repeated in a softer voice, "No, I do not."

Glendale felt as if a giant weight had been removed from his soul. He had told himself that she did not love, could not love, the middle-aged Cit, but it was a relief to hear it from her own lips.

Gazing down at her face, he realized how wonderful it felt to hold her in his arms. "I refuse to give you up," he warned. Jane's lips parted in surprise, offering an unconscious invitation. He couldn't resist the temptation, and bent his head down to kiss her.

Her lips were soft and warm, just as he had known they would be. Jane was passive at first, but soon began to respond to the insistent demands of his lips. He wrapped her arms about him, and deepened the kiss, savoring her innocent response.

It was with regret that he finally ended the kiss. Jane drew back, her eyes wide with passionate wonder. She reached up one hand and tentatively touched her mouth, where his lips had been.

"We were meant to be together," Glendale reassured her.

Jane shook her head as if to clear it. She leaned backwards, breaking free from his embrace. "This changes nothing," she said, rising swiftly and seating herself on the opposite bench.

How could she be unaffected after the kiss they had shared? "Nothing? This changes everything," Glendale thundered. "I love you, you widgeon. And I know you love me. And we're going to be married."

Jane's small smile did not reach her eyes. "Only you

would make a declaration of love sound like an ultimatum." At least she had not denied that she loved him in return. Her smile vanished, leaving only determination in its place. Glendale had the sinking feeling that he was not going to like what she said next. "I am promised to Mr. Whitmore, and I intend to honor my promise."

This couldn't be happening. It wasn't possible. No woman could be that pigheaded and stubborn. "But you can't marry him. You don't love him. You told me yourself."

"Mr. Whitmore knew that I didn't love him when he made his offer. He offered a marriage of convenience."

"A marriage of convenience? James Whitmore doesn't want a wife, he wants a brood mare." Jane flushed, and Glendale knew his words stung. "And have you thought about the sons you are supposed to give him? This isn't an arrangement where you each go your separate ways. Have you thought what it will be like when Mr. Whitmore claims his marital rights? Have you thought about how it will feel when he kisses you? When he climbs into your bed, and—"

"Stop this!" Jane yelled. "Stop being cruel. It isn't like that."

"Then what is it?" Glendale asked, trying his best to sound understanding. Why couldn't she see what was so obvious to him? Her hesitation was driving him crazy.

"Mr. Whitmore came to my aid when no one else would. He has been very good to me and my family. I can't cry off now. He doesn't deserve to be treated in such a shabby fashion."

"And what about us? Are you going to ruin our lives, out of some misguided sense of gratitude?"

Jane was furious over Glendale's high-handedness. How dare he proclaim himself in love with her, as if that fact alone solved everything? Didn't he realize that it was too late? "It is too late," Jane said aloud.

"Is it? Or are you just too stubborn to admit that you've made a mistake?" Glendale demanded. His chilly tones were a stark contrast to the anger in his eyes.

Jane opened her mouth to defend herself, and then closed it with a snap as she forgot what she wanted to say. She was doing the right thing. Marrying Mr. Whitmore was the only honorable choice, wasn't it? If only Glendale would give her time to think. But the more he shouted, the angrier she became.

Glendale tried a new tack. "I don't think I could bear to see you again as Mrs. Whitmore," he said.

Jane blinked as she considered the notion. Glendale was right. It was impossible for them to remain simply friends. And while many ladies of the *ton* conducted discreet affairs, Jane couldn't picture herself and Glendale in such a sordid relationship.

How would it be to never see Matthew again, except as a distant stranger at public events? Never to have the warmth of his companionship? Losing him again would hurt more than before, for this time she had no shield of righteous anger to hide behind. Even thinking about it made her heart sore.

"Enough," Jane said. Glendale was right. It was time to be her mother's daughter, and to trust her heart instead of her head. The demands of convention and obligation meant little when measured against the cost of losing Matthew forever. Slighting Mr. Whitmore would be hard, but far less difficult than condemning them both to a marriage based on a lie. For how could she promise to honor and obey one man, when she loved another?

"Enough what?"

Jane essayed a smile, but she knew it was a weak effort. "Enough quarreling. For once, you are right. Marrying Whitmore would be the biggest mistake of my life."

Glendale reached over and grasped her hands in his. "Does this mean that you'll marry me?"

"Yes. If only because no one else would put up with your rag manners," she replied, trying to interject a note of lightness. She knew she should be feeling joyful, but she merely felt drained. There was a sense of relief at having made a decision, mixed with dread at having to tell Mr. Whitmore.

"You won't regret this. I swear to you I'll make you happy," Glendale promised. And by the smile on his face, he was feeling enough joy for both of them.

Chapter Fifteen

Mr. Whitmore arrived that afternoon, in response to Jane's frantic summons. They exchanged greetings, and Jane enquired after his health. She then lapsed into silence, uncertain of how to begin.

"Your note said it was urgent," Mr. Whitmore prompted.

Jane nodded in reply.

"Is there something amiss with Lady Barton?"

Well, yes, there was, but she could hardly tell him that Lady Barton had taken to her bed with a fit of megrims, once she learned that Jane was to marry Lord Glendale.

"No, my aunt is quite well." Jane drew a deep breath, steadying her courage. There was no gentle way to do this, so she should just tell him the truth. "I needed to speak to you about a more personal matter. About us. And our marriage."

"Indeed?"

Oh dear, this was going to be even more awkward than she had feared. Mr. Whitmore wore an expression of gentle interest. He clearly had no idea of what she was going to say next.

Jane fixed her gaze on her hands, which were tightly clenched together. Maybe if she didn't look at him, it would be easier. "I have given this much thought, and I am afraid that I can no longer accept your offer of marriage. You have been most kind and generous, and I am not worthy—"

"It is Lord Glendale, isn't it?" Mr. Whitmore interrupted.

"How did you know?"

Mr. Whitmore gave a sad smile. "I always knew that you held a *tendre* for him. And from his behavior the other night, I suspected that he returned your feelings. When Lord David Cartland made a disparaging remark about you, Glendale came close to calling him out."

It was gratifying to know that Glendale had leapt to her defense, but how mortifying it must have been for Mr. Whitmore. Jane couldn't help but feel sorry for him. Mr. Whitmore was truly the innocent party in this affair, and it wasn't right that he be hurt.

"Mr. Whitmore, I have treated you rather shabbily. I am ashamed when I think of how good you have been to me and my family. I don't know how we will ever repay you."

"Don't condemn yourself," Mr. Whitmore said. "It may have all worked out for the best. In the last weeks I have had my own doubts about the wisdom of starting a new family at my age."

Her erstwhile suitor appeared resigned rather than angry. Perhaps Mr. Whitmore wasn't just being kind, and he truly had second thoughts about the marriage.

"I take it that Lord Glendale has offered you marriage?" Mr. Whitmore asked.

"Yes," Jane said.

Mr. Whitmore rose from his seat. He took her right

hand in farewell. "Then I wish you both much happiness," he said.

Mr. Whitmore was kindness itself. It wasn't fair that he should be hurt. She wanted to jump up, to tell him that it was all a horrible mistake, and that she would be pleased to be his wife after all. But Jane kept silent. She had always known that Mr. Whitmore was an estimable gentleman. But she loved another, and nothing could change that.

He paused at the door, and then turned back to face her. "Did I ever tell you that my sister's youngest boy is named after me?"

"No," Jane said, confused by this change of topic.

"They call him James Mallery. He seems a likely enough lad, and I've often thought he would have a good head for the business. Perhaps it's time that I sent for him," Mr. Whitmore said, as if thinking aloud. Then he gave a her a half bow and departed.

Jane didn't know how long she remained sitting there, lost in thought. She might have stayed there all day, if Browning hadn't shown in another caller.

"Matthew!" she cried, jumping up and running across the room.

Glendale gave her a quick embrace. "I know what we agreed, but I couldn't stay away any longer."

It was so good to see him, to have him hold her. Just the sight of him made her feel better. "It's all right," Jane reassured him. "Mr. Whitmore just left."

Glendale took a step back, so he could look at her. "Did you tell him?"

"Yes," Jane said, saddened by the memory of the conversation. "He was so good about it. It just doesn't seem fair." She rested her head against Glendale's shoulder, which gave her an excellent view of Browning's apoplectic expression.

"You know that I will repay him," Glendale said.

"Of course. But it isn't the money. He is such a nice man," Jane tried to explain.

"Well, you can't marry both of us," Glendale replied, a hint of exasperation in his tone.

The thought prompted her to giggle. "I know that, silly." It was incredible. She knew that she should be sorry for hurting Mr. Whitmore, but all she could feel was an overwhelming happiness. Matthew loves me, and we are to be married, she told herself. Surely there could be no greater joy.

"I love you, and we're going to be married," she repeated aloud, for Glendale's benefit.

"There's no need to sound so amazed," Glendale said. Behind him, the imperturbable Browning stood gaping, his mouth open.

"Married?" the butler croaked.

Glendale gave Jane a final squeeze and then removed his arms. "We're scandalizing the servants," he told her, taking a step back. "Why don't you invite me in?"

"Oh, yes," Jane said. "Do come in and take a seat. We have so much to talk about." She took a wicked delight in seeing Browning's discomfiture.

She had taken but two steps when the front knocker sounded. Jane paused, wondering who on earth would be calling at this hour. Browning rushed over to open the door. Jane heard the sound of excited chatter. Those voices sounded familiar. It couldn't be, could it?

"Jane, Jane, where are you?" Little Michael burst past the butler and came running into the foyer. His speed proved his undoing, for he slipped on the marble and fell on his backside. Undaunted he scrambled back up. "Jane!" he yelled.

"I take it the family has arrived?" Glendale asked. There was no time to reply.

"Here I am," Jane said, stepping out into the hallway. "But what are you doing here?"

Michael stopped and stared at her. "Janey?" he asked. Jane leaned over and picked him up. Ouch. Either Michael had put on weight, or she was no longer as strong as she used to be. "Yes, it is me," Jane said. She kissed Michael on the cheek, and then set him down.

Michael wiped his cheek with the back of his hand. "I *knew* it was you," he said. Then he rushed back through the open door. "I found her!" he yelled.

The rest of her family came in through the open door. Jane was rapidly surrounded, lost in a flurry of hugs and heartfelt greetings. It was all noise and confusion, and it was wonderful. "Oh Mama, I am so happy to see you," Jane said, when Lady Alice finally appeared, bringing up the tail of her brood. "But what are you all doing here? We didn't expect you for days yet."

Lady Alice scrutinized Jane. "Well, you look astonishingly well." Taking off her cape and hat, she handed them to one of the footmen who had appeared, drawn by all the noise.

"Mama, Mama, doesn't Jane look elegant? I hardly recognized her," Katherine remarked.

"I'm hungry, Mama," Jonathan complained.

Everyone was talking at once, not waiting for an answer. Jane spun around, trying to keep an eye on the littlest ones. Where had Michael gone off to?

"Children," Lady Alice said, holding up one hand. A miraculous silence reigned. "You, sir, what is your name?"

"Browning, milady," the butler replied, with an attempt at his old dignity. The events of the last hour had put a serious dent in his composure.

"Very well, Browning. See that tea is served in . . ."

"The morning room," Jane suggested helpfully.

"See that tea is served in the morning room. Then inform Lady Barton that her sister has arrived." Lady Alice's gaze swept the hall, counting her flock. Apparently she came up one short. "Michael, come out at once," she ordered.

Michael obediently emerged from his hiding place behind a particularly ugly statue.

"Children, take off your coats and give them to the footmen. Then follow Mr. Browning, and he'll see that you have some tea."

Heartened by the prospect of refreshment, the children were quick to comply. Only Ellen demurred. "But what about Jane?" she asked.

"Jane and I have to talk" Lady Alice replied. "We will be along later."

In no time at all, the children cast off their outer garments and followed Browning upstairs. The foyer seemed much too quiet, with only the three of them remaining. Glendale, who had stood observing the whole proceedings from the sidelines, now came forward.

"Mama, may I present Lord Glendale?"

Glendale lifted her mother's hand and raised it to his lips. "A pleasure to meet you, Lady Alice. I can see now where Jane gets her beauty."

Lady Alice smiled, not immune to the flattery of a handsome man. "The pleasure is mine, Lord Glendale. My daughter has written so much about you."

Glendale shot Jane a look. Jane could feel her cheeks heating in mortification, as she tried frantically to remember just what it was that she had written.

"You must be tired after your long journey," Glendale said diplomatically. "I will take my leave now, so you can rest and have a chance to talk with your daughter."

"No, please stay a moment," Lady Alice said. Then she looked over at Jane. "I came because of your letters. You seemed unhappy, and I had the feeling that you were about to make a terrible mistake." Her mother gave Jane a searching look that made Jane feel as if she were six years old again. "But perhaps I was mistaken. You seem quite well."

Jane didn't know how to break the news. And Glendale was no help. He just stood there, carefully neutral. Probably wondering just what it was she had written about him. Well, it served him right.

"I look forward to meeting your fiancé Mr. Whitmore," Lady Alice said finally.

"I'm afraid that's not possible," Jane said.

"Not possible? Has something happened to him?" her mother demanded.

Glendale finally took pity on her. He moved over to stand next to Jane, and wrapped one arm affectionately about her waist. "What your daughter is trying to say is that there has been a change of plans. She's going to marry me, instead."

Lady Alice beamed.

"She's marrying Lord Glendale! I told you she would," Bobby whispered loudly. Jane turned and saw the children lined up on the staircase. So much for privacy. Apparently her brothers and sisters had forsaken the promised nourishment in favor of witnessing the unfolding drama.

"Are you sure you are ready to take us on?" Lady Alice asked drily. "They're not usually this well behaved."

"I can think of nothing I want more," Glendale replied.

Jane's heart swelled with happiness. "And I love you, too, Matthew Kingsley," she declared. Then, surprising herself with her daring, she turned and gave him a kiss. She intended only a quick brush of their lips, but Glendale had other intentions, cupping his hands around her face, and giving her all his attention.

"Oh, isn't it too romantic," Rosemarie sighed. And Jane, caught up in Glendale's kisses, silently agreed.

The children clattered down the stairs, eager to join in the celebrations. Glendale released her with a pleasing show of reluctance. "We'll finish this later," he promised.

"Congratulations, sir," Dick said, sticking out his hand for Glendale to shake. "I am sure my sister will make you very happy."

"You mean he will make her happy," Bobby countered.

Glendale shook both their hands solemnly. "I am certain we will do our best to make each other happy," he promised.

"May I present the rest of my family?" Jane offered. "You've met the twins already. This is Rosemarie, who's next in age to me. Then there's Katherine, Emily, Ellen, Jonathan, and Michael our baby."

"I'm not a baby," Michael insisted.

"Does this mean we're rich? We won't be poor again?" Ellen asked anxiously. She couldn't have been more than nine or ten, but for all her youth she looked like a miniature of his Jane, right down to the way her brow furrowed when she was worried.

Glendale hastened to reassure the child. "It means that you will be part of my family, and that I will take care of everyone."

"If we're rich, then I want a pony," Jonathan said.

Why not? His own happiness was such that he felt an urge to share it. "Everyone can have a pony," Glendale promised recklessly.

The children cheered. "Matthew, you mustn't spoil them," Jane protested.

"I hardly think a few ponies are likely to spoil them," Glendale countered.

"I don't like horses. May I have a new dress instead?" Emily asked. "I'll be fifteen next month."

"Children, children," Lady Alice admonished. "You mustn't be so forward. What will Lord Glendale think of you?"

"Jane, next year may Rosemarie and I come to London with you?" Katherine begged. "It's not fair that you had all the fun."

Glendale and Jane shared amused glances. Not all of her season had been fun, but she wouldn't have missed it for the world.

"Everyone can have whatever their hearts desire," Glendale promised. "But in return you must give me what I want."

"And what does Lord Glendale want?" Jane enquired.

He gave her a look that heated her blood. "A few minutes alone with my intended."

Lady Alice was quick to take the hint, rising and heading for the door. "Now come along," she said. "Tea is waiting upstairs, and they'll be plenty of time to pester Jane later."

For once her siblings did as they were told. In a twinkling of an eye the room was empty, and they were left alone.

"I believe this is where we left off," Glendale said, gathering Jane in his arms. She sank eagerly into his embrace, her eyes sparkling with delight as his head bent down to claim her lips with his own.